漂鳥集
Stray Birds

泰戈爾 著
Rabindranath Tagore

余淑慧、余淑娟 譯

關於「漂鳥」——代出版說明

文／余淑慧、余淑娟

　　泰戈爾這部詩集的英文原名是 *Stray Birds*，意思是「離群的鳥」或「流離失所的鳥」。[1]

　　一九二二年，鄭振鐸首度完整譯介這部詩集，把書名譯爲《飛鳥集》。四〇至七〇年代，糜文開和周策縱分別譯成《漂鳥集》和《失群的鳥》。二〇〇二年，再有羅青的選譯本《單飛集》。與此同時，坊間也出現各式各樣的版本，有的另訂書名（如「泰戈爾的詩」），更常見的是沿用糜文開的譯法，早年甚至也有出版社把鄭振鐸的版本改名爲《漂鳥集》。可見歷來台灣讀者熟知且喜愛的譯名是「漂鳥」。

　　「漂鳥」，意指漂泊各地的鳥類。至於糜文開爲何選用「漂鳥」一詞來對譯？其實過程頗爲曲折。據糜文開的序，他把詩集譯成「漂鳥」，最主要的原因是覺得「飛鳥」或當時流行的「迷鳥」這兩個譯詞不甚妥當，在研究了原著的詩意與背景之後，他決定譯爲「漂鳥」。如此對譯的

1　查閱線上《牛津英文字典》（http://en.oxforddictionaries.com），"stray" 作形容詞用，有兩個定義。第一個是 "not in the right place" 和 "separated from the group or target"，意指某事物「並未處在本來應該在的地方」或「偏離了所屬的群體或預定的目標」。第二個定義是 "having no home or having wandered away from home"，字典特別標明該定義用在馴養的動物身上（of a domestic animal），意指那些「沒有居所或離開了居所的」動物，如流浪犬（stray dogs）；這字的同義詞有 "homeless"，"wandering" 等，含有「無家可歸」、「流離失所」的意涵。

理由有二：第一，就文化上來說，印度人本來就很敬重漂泊四方的流浪者。印度修行者的人生可分為淨行、居家、修行、苦行四階段，修行者在完成就學、工作、成家、孩子長大成人等世俗責任之後，即可離家雲遊，展開敬神的苦修生活，例如《漂鳥集》第 2 首就描寫了詩人對流浪者的嚮往；再加上印度當時還有「流浪詩人」挨家挨戶吟唱印度兩大史詩，可見印度人「對雲遊的重視，對漂泊者的尊敬」。第二個理由是，糜文開在查找了動物學的專業書籍後，得知會「唱歌的鶯類」就是「漂鳥之一種」，與第 1 首的「詩句完全符合」，於是下定決心，把詩集名譯為《漂鳥集》。[2]

這篇譯序，我們讀來心有戚戚焉。遙想嚴復當年為了譯"introduction"一字，遍查內、外典籍，最後終於求得「導言」一詞對譯。據〈天演論・譯例言〉，「導言」的「一名之立」，嚴復竟「旬月踟躕」，推敲了大半個月。糜文開之翻譯「漂鳥」，其所花費的心力與查找工夫，與嚴復的「旬月踟躕」竟不相上下，讀來令人十分感動。我們思前想後，覺得《漂鳥集》一名既富有文化內涵，在中文語境裡又兼具譯事／譯史的傳承意味，因而決定沿用此一譯名，以示對於譯事前輩的敬重。

2　見〈漂鳥集序〉，收在糜文開、糜榴麗、裴普賢譯，《泰戈爾詩集》（台北市：三民書局，2013 年），頁 5。

Stray Birds

1

夏日，漂泊的群鳥來我窗前歌唱，飛離。
秋天，黃葉翩然飄落，無歌，只有一聲嘆息。[1]

STRAY birds of summer come to my window to sing and fly
away.
And yellow leaves of autumn, which have no songs, flutter
and fall there with a sigh.

2

行旅世間的流浪者啊，請在我的詩裡留下你們的足跡。

O TROUPE of little vagrants of the world, leave your
footprints in my words.

3

世界在戀人面前揭下浩瀚無垠的面具；
變得小小的，如歌，亦如永恆的一吻。

THE world puts off its mask of vastness to its lover.
It becomes small as one song, as one kiss of the eternal.

1　這大概是泰戈爾最著名的一首詩了，雖只有兩行，但結構謹嚴，色彩華麗，
　　宛如一方經緯縝密的美麗織錦。此種縝密之感來自對比手法之運用。首先
　　是語彙的對比：夏日對秋天，漂鳥對落葉；飛離對飄落，歌唱對嘆息。其
　　次是空間或動線的對比：漂鳥的飛離是水平動線，落葉飄落在地則是垂直
　　動線，如此上下兩句之間產生了動線上的對比。英文的聲韻結構也是一種
　　對比，如第一句用了頭韻 / s/（[s]tray birds of summer），第二句在描寫葉
　　落的兩個主要動詞也用了頭韻 / f/（flutter and fall）；在聽覺效果上，前一
　　句讀來舒緩綿長，後一句讀來稍微短促，形成音效上的對比或者甚至帶出
　　意義上的對比，如漂鳥的飛離對照落葉的停留，漂鳥的歌唱對應落葉的嘆
　　息，前後兩句因此交相映照，彷彿有餘韻不斷繚繞。（編按：本書所有腳
　　注皆為譯者注。）

4

正是大地自己的淚，讓她常保笑靨如花。

IT is the tears of the earth that keep her smiles in bloom.

5

大漠燃起熱情如火，渴求一葉小草的愛；小草只搖一搖頭，笑著飛走了。

THE mighty desert is burning for the love of a blade of grass who shakes her head and laughs and flies away.

6

如果你因錯過太陽而流淚，你也將錯過與繁星的交會。[2]

IF you shed tears when you miss the sun, you also miss the stars.

7

舞動的流水啊，你途中的沙礫渴求你的歌，你的舞。
你是否願意擔起跛足的沙礫，與之一起踏上旅途？

THE sands in your way beg for your song and your
movement, dancing water.
Will you carry the burden of their lameness?

---

2 這首詩有兩個 "miss" 字，這個字當動詞用，除了「錯過」，也有「思念」
之意。主句的 "miss" 取「錯過」之意大致沒問題，但是附屬子句裡的 "miss"
卻兩個意思皆可通，除了「錯過」，也可以譯成「如果你因思念太陽而流
淚，你也將錯過與繁星的交會」（淚眼模糊，當然看不到星星）。語意的
多重性是泰戈爾創造詩意的其中一個手法，英語讀者一讀即可體會其妙處，
但是翻譯涉及選擇，而且通常只能選擇其中一個意思，其他可能的意思就
不得不割愛，或另以其他方式加以解釋或說明了（例如這裡的腳注）。

8

她憂傷的臉縈繞在我夢裡，猶如夜雨淅淅瀝瀝。

HER wistful face haunts my dreams like the rain at night.

9

曾經我們夢見你我形同陌路。
如今醒來，發現彼此原是好相識。

ONCE we dreamt that we were strangers.
We wake up to find that we were dear to each other.

10

我心中的憂傷已漸漸平息，猶如樹木默然靜立的林中黃昏。

SORROW is hushed into peace in my heart like the evening
among the silent trees.

11

是誰伸出纖指輕輕，如微風拂過我心，奏起一波波漣漪的樂音。

SOME unseen fingers, like idle breeze, are playing upon my heart the music of the ripples.

12

「大海，你在說甚麼啊？」
「亙久的疑問。」
「藍天啊，你如何應答？」
「永恆的沉默。」

"WHAT language is thine, O sea?"
"The language of eternal question."
"What language is thy answer, O sky? "
"The language of eternal silence."

13

我的心啊，請聆聽世界的低語！世界正在對你表示愛意。

LISTEN, my heart, to the whispers of the world with which it makes love to you.

14

造物的奧祕猶如暗夜的黑——廣大無垠。
知識帶來的許多錯覺，就像晨間的霧。[3]

THE mystery of creation is like the darkness of night — it is great.
Delusions of knowledge are like the fog of the morning.

15

別把你的愛安置在懸崖上，就只因爲懸崖高峭。

DO not seat your love upon a precipice because it is high.

16

今晨我坐在窗前；世界像個旅人走來，停駐片刻，朝我點點頭，就逕自走開。

I SIT at my window this morning where the world like a passer-by stops for a moment, nods to me and goes.

17

瑣碎的思緒是葉子的沙沙聲，在我腦海裡輕輕說著歡樂的絮語。

THESE little thoughts are the rustle of leaves; they have their whisper of joy in my mind.

3　我們以為知識可以為我們解惑，讓我們了解世間萬象的奧祕；但是知識是人為的，有時也會給我們帶來「我們知道這個那個」的錯覺，詩人認為這種種錯覺就像晨間的霧，有時反而讓人看不清楚。在這首詩裡，詩人把人的知識與造物的奧祕做一對比，當然我們也可以進一步將詩意引申理解為「不變的無限」與「變化的有限」之間的差異或對照。

18

眞正的你，你看不見；你看見的，只是你的影子。

WHAT you are you do not see, what you see is your shadow.

19

神啊，我的願望是一群傻瓜，只曉得對祢的歌大聲叫囂。
讓我只管聆聽就好。

MY wishes are fools, they shout across thy songs, my Master.
Let me but listen.

20

我無法挑選那最好的；
那最好的挑選了我。

I CANNOT choose the best.
The best chooses me.

21

把燈籠揹在身後的人，讓影子投落在他們身前。

THEY throw their shadows before them who carry their
lantern on their back.

22

我存在——這是永恆的驚喜，生命的驚喜。

THAT I exist is a perpetual surprise which is life.

23

「我們是沙沙作響的葉，我們用聲音回應暴風雨的吹襲；
可你是誰啊，怎麼如此沉默？」
「我只是一朵花。」

"WE, the rustling leaves, have a voice that answers the storms,
but who are you so silent?"
"I am a mere flower."

24

休息與工作相依，猶如眼瞼與眼睛相屬。

REST belongs to the work as the eyelids to the eyes.

25

人類是初生的孩子，其力量寓於成長。

MAN is a born child, his power is the power of growth.

26

神期待我們對祂贈送的繁花有所回應，太陽與大地則都是祂的恩賜。

GOD expects answers for the flowers he sends us, not for the sun and the earth.

27

陽光像赤裸的孩子，在綠葉之間歡樂嬉戲，渾然不知人可是會撒謊的。

THE light that plays, like a naked child, among the green leaves happily knows not that man can lie.

28

美啊，去愛裡尋找妳自己，別理會鏡子的諂媚。

O BEAUTY, find thyself in love, not in the flattery of thy mirror.

29

我的心在世界的海岸拍起浪花朵朵，含著淚在岸上題字：「我愛你。」

MY heart beats her waves at the shore of the world and writes upon it her signature in tears with the words, "I love thee."

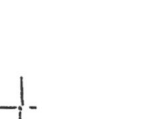

30

「月啊，你爲何在此等待？」

「爲了向太陽敬禮，給太陽讓路。」

"MOON, for what do you wait?"

"To salute the sun for whom I must make way."

31

樹木長高，枝枒探向我的窗，就像瘖啞大地充滿渴望的聲音。

THE trees come up to my window like the yearning voice of the dumb earth.

32

神創造的早晨，每一天都教祂感到新奇。

HIS own mornings are new surprises to God.

33

生命在世人的諸多要求裡找到財富，在愛情的種種索求中
找到價值。

LIFE finds its wealth by the claims of the world, and its worth
by the claims of love.

34

乾涸的河床發現，沒人會爲了他的過往而對他說聲謝謝。[4]

THE dry river-bed finds no thanks for its past.

4　這首詩把河流擬人化，並以平淡的語氣，描述河床乾涸之後的感慨。河床
　　的所謂的「過往」，指河床裡還有水的那些日子；那些日子裡，他是一條
　　河，他對人類貢獻很多，人類對他也心懷感激。如今河水流盡，河床乾涸，
　　河床仍然是同一個河床，只是乾涸之後的河床發現沒有人會想到他的過去，
　　或想到過去的他曾是一條河，從而對他此時此刻的狀況產生同情或至少心
　　懷感激。詩中的動詞用第三人稱現在式，表示乾涸河床的這一感慨是恆在
　　的，亦即河流乾涸之後，狀況就一直是如此。這裡有個隱藏的今昔對比，
　　雖然河流乾涸在農業社會是個常見的現象，但是透過河床的角度把這現象
　　說出來，仍讓人有不勝唏噓之感。此外，乾涸的河床亦可視爲隱喻，喻指
　　風燭殘年的老人。若是可以如此閱讀，則就更令人心生感慨了。

35

飛鳥但願自己變成雲；雲但願自己化成飛鳥。

THE bird wishes it were a cloud. The cloud wishes it were a bird.

36

瀑布如此歌唱：「一旦找到自由，我就找到自己的歌。」

THE waterfall sings, "I find my song, when I find my freedom."

37

我說不上來，何以我這顆心在沉默裡頹喪。

不外是爲了那些我不曾要，無從知曉或無從記得的小需小
求。

I CANNOT tell why this heart languishes in silence.
It is for small needs it never asks, or knows or remembers.

38

女人，妳在家中來回走動料理家務，妳的舉手投足有如山
泉的歌唱，潺潺在溪石之間。

WOMAN, when you move about in your household service
your limbs sing like a hill stream among its pebbles.

39

太陽朝西橫渡大海，向東方獻上最後的禮讚。

THE sun goes to cross the Western sea, leaving its last salutation to the East.

40

別因食慾不振，就責怪你的食物無味。

DO not blame your food because you have no appetite.

41

樹木就像大地的渴望，踮起腳尖，遙遙窺向天堂。

THE trees, like the longings of the earth, stand a-tiptoe to peep at the heaven.

42

你對我微微一笑，甚麼也沒說；不知為何，我覺得這一刻我已等待許久。

YOU smiled and talked to me of nothing and I felt that for this I had been waiting long.

43

水中的游魚沉默無聲，陸上的百獸吵鬧喧騰，空中的飛鳥自由歌唱。
但人類心中自有大海的沉默，陸地的喧騰，空中的樂音。[5]

THE fish in the water is silent, the animal on the earth is noisy, the bird in the air is singing.
But Man has in him the silence of the sea, the noise of the earth and the music of the air.

5　這首詩主要表達一個概念：人心本自俱足。詩人以排比的手法，為我們描繪了三幅涵蓋海陸空的華麗場景，一幅比一幅壯闊，一幅比一幅高揚。不過，第二句句首輕輕安置的一個單音節字「但」（But），卻把前面所有的沉默、喧騰或樂音全部扭轉方向，收攝於人的內心，並且小小地排比開來，使上下兩句形成呼應，也形成強烈的對比。

44

紅塵倥傯，在徬徨不捨的心上奏起憂傷的樂音。

THE world rushes on over the strings of the lingering heart making the music of sadness.

45

奉武器爲神明的人，一旦武器獲勝，他自己就落敗了。

HE has made his weapons his gods. When his weapons win he is defeated himself.

46

神藉由創造，尋找祂自己。

GOD finds himself by creating.

影子垂下面紗，輕悄柔順地跟著光，步步無聲，步步都是愛。

SHADOW, with her veil drawn, follows Light in secret meekness, with her silent steps of love.

48

星星才不在乎自己看起來像螢火蟲。

THE stars are not afraid to appear like fireflies.

49

我與權力之輪無關，我與所有被權力之輪碾壓的生靈同在；
為此──我向祢致謝。

I THANK thee that I am none of the wheels of power but I am
one with the living creatures that are crushed by it.

50

敏銳但狹隘的心靈執著於每一點，無法向前。

THE mind, sharp but not broad, sticks at every point but does
not move.

51

你的偶像業已粉碎，化為塵土──這證明了神的塵土比你
的偶像偉大。

YOUR idol is shattered in the dust to prove that God's dust is
greater than your idol.

52

人掙扎著走完一生，不是在生命史上亮個相而已。

MAN does not reveal himself in his history, he struggles up through it.

53

玻璃燈責罵陶器喚他作堂表親。看到明月東升，玻璃燈立刻和悅地招呼明月：「親愛的，我最親愛的姐妹。」

WHILE the glass lamp rebukes the earthen for calling it cousin,
the moon rises, and the glass lamp, with a bland smile, calls her, "My dear, dear sister."

54

就像海鷗遇見海浪，我們相遇，我們相知相惜。海鷗飛去，
海浪捲退，我們分離。

LIKE the meeting of the seagulls and the waves we meet and
come near. The seagulls fly off, the waves roll away and we
depart.

55

一日的工作完畢，我像拖上沙灘的小船，躺在黃昏裡靜聽
潮汐的舞曲。

MY day is done, and I am like a boat drawn on the beach,
listening to the dance-music of the tide in the evening.

56

生命是天賜的禮物；我們藉由奉獻生命，獲得這份贈禮。[6]

LIFE is given to us, we earn it by giving it.

57

我們越謙卑，越接近偉大。

WE come nearest to the great when we are great in humility.

58

孔雀拖著沉重的長尾，麻雀對此深表同情。

THE sparrow is sorry for the peacock at the burden of its tail.

6　英文原文在兩個子句裡分別使用動詞 "to give" 的分詞形式（giving）和被動
　　分詞形式（given），一來符合文法的要求，二來創造語言趣味，讀來既有
　　連貫，亦富變化，且與詩意若有重合，十分生動巧妙。

59

永遠別害怕那些霎時與剎那啊──永恆之聲如是歌唱。

NEVER be afraid of the moments — thus sings the voice of the everlasting.

60

颶風在無路之處找尋最短的路，不意卻在無何有之處覷見歸宿。[7]

THE hurricane seeks the shortest road by the no-road, and suddenly ends its search in the Nowhere.

61

朋友，就著我的酒杯喝吧。
一倒入他人的酒杯，杯沿的酒花就化成了泡影。

TAKE my wine in my own cup, friend.
It loses its wreath of foam when poured into that of others.

62

爲了得到不完美的愛，完美豔抹濃妝，把自己裝扮得漂漂亮亮。

THE Perfect decks itself in beauty for the love of the Imperfect.

63

神對世人說：「爲了醫治你，所以傷害你；因爲愛惜你，所以懲罰你。」

GOD says to man,"I heal you therefore I hurt, love you therefore punish."

7　擬人化是泰戈爾創造詩意的常用手法。這裡把颶風比喻爲急切的尋路人（或歸人），這颶風在無路之處（the no-road）尋找最短的路（the shortest road），不料卻在一個甚麼也不是的地方（the Nowhere）終止追尋。這裡的 no-road 和 shortest road 關連，而 no-road 又和下一句的 Nowhere 關連，三者相互呼應，環環相扣，彷彿一條由文字打造的路徑。這樣的文字遊戲常見於此詩集。譯文的「無何有之處」借用莊子的「無何有之鄉」（無實有的境界），扣住「無」（no）字，重新創造一「無路之處」與之關連。另外，「無路之處」還可以和「最短的路」產生「路－最短的路－無路之處」的連結，如此一來，英文裡的兩個關連都照顧到了，雖然「最短的路」譯成「捷徑」可能會比「最短的路」簡潔，但是為了詩中的文字遊戲，只得做此小小犧牲。

64

感謝燭火的光，但可別忘了始終佇立在陰影裡的燭臺。

THANK the flame for its light, but do not forget the lamp-holder standing in the shade with constancy of patience.

65

小草啊，儘管步履碎細，你卻擁有腳下的大地。

TINY grass, your steps are small, but you possess the earth under your tread.

66

小小花從蓓蕾中綻放，對世界呼叫道：「親愛的世界，千萬別凋謝啊！」

THE infant flower opens its bud and cries, "Dear World, please do not fade."

67

神會對偉大的帝國心生厭倦，對小小的花朵卻永懷眷戀。

GOD grows weary of great kingdoms, but never of little flowers.

68

錯誤禁不起挫敗，真理卻禁得起。

WRONG cannot afford defeat but Right can.

69

瀑布如此歌唱：「儘管斗升之水即能止渴，我卻樂於獻出所有。」

"I GIVE my whole water in joy," sings the waterfall, "though little of it is enough for the thirsty."

70

這般永無止盡，這般歡喜雀躍地噴灑水花的泉源，究竟是在何方？

WHERE is the fountain that throws up these flowers in a ceaseless outbreak of ecstasy?

71

樵夫的斧頭向大樹討根斧柄。
大樹慨然應允。

THE woodcutter's axe begged for its handle from the tree.
The tree gave it.

72

失偶的黃昏披著雨霧交織的面紗，我孤寂的心，感覺到她的嘆息。

IN my solitude of heart I feel the sigh of this widowed
evening veiled with mist and rain.

73

貞潔是一種財富，其源頭是豐沛的愛。

CHASTITY is a wealth that comes from abundance of love.

74

雲霧像愛，流連在群山的心間，牽引出層層美的驚喜。

THE mist, like love, plays upon the heart of the hills and brings out surprises of beauty.

75

我們誤讀了世界，倒說世界欺騙我們。

WE read the world wrong and say that it deceives us.

76

風就像詩人，飛越海洋，穿過森林，尋找自己的聲音。

THE poet wind is out over the sea and the forest to seek his own voice.

77

每個孩子的誕生都捎來一則訊息：神對人類尚未感到絕望。

EVERY child comes with the message that God is not yet
discouraged of man.

78

小草在地上尋找同伴；
大樹往天空探求孤獨。[8]

THE grass seeks her crowd in the earth.
The tree seeks his solitude of the sky.

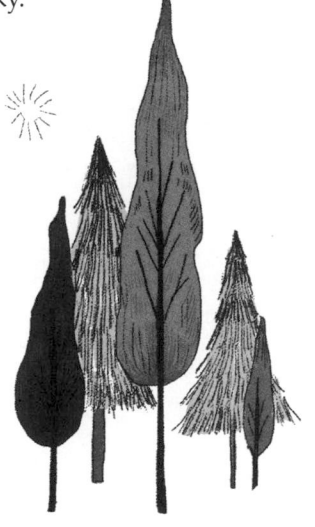

8　這首詩的原文很清楚點出小草和大樹的性別。如要在中文翻譯裡清楚顯示
　　性別，則這首詩可能要譯為：小草在地上尋找她的同伴；大樹往天空探求
　　他的孤獨。

79

人會自設障礙，堵自己的去路。

MAN barricades against himself.

80

朋友，你的聲音在我心裡徘徊，就像濤聲隱隱，迴盪在靜靜聆聽的松林之間。

YOUR voice, my friend, wanders in my heart, like the muffled sound of the sea among these listening pines.

81

那不可見的幽黯之火究係何物！迸散的火花竟然就是繁星？

WHAT is this unseen flame of darkness whose sparks are the stars?

82

願生之美，有如夏日繁花；願死之豔，恰似秋天黃葉。

LET life be beautiful like summer flowers and death like autumn leaves.

83

想要行善的人，上前敲門；樂於行善的人，看到開啓的門。

HE who wants to do good knocks at the gate; he who loves finds the gate open.

84

在死亡裡，多化成一；在生命裡，一化成多。
神若死去，世間宗教亦將同歸於一。

IN death the many becomes one; in life the one becomes many.
Religion will be one when God is dead.

85

藝術家熱愛大自然，藝術家因此是大自然的奴隸，也是大自然的主人。

THE artist is the lover of Nature, therefore he is her slave and her master.

86

「果子啊，你離我多遠？」
「花朵啊，我就藏在你心田。」

"HOW far are you from me, O Fruit?"
"I am hidden in your heart, O Flower."

87

這份盼望只留給他──白天看不到，但是夜裡感覺得到的他。

THIS longing is for the one who is felt in the dark, but not seen in the day.

88

露珠對湖水如是說：「你是荷葉下面的大露珠，我是荷葉上面的小露珠。」

"YOU are the big drop of dew under the lotus leaf, I am the smaller one on its upper side," said the dewdrop to the lake.

89

只要能確保劍鋒的利，劍鞘並不介意自己的鈍。

THE scabbard is content to be dull when it protects the keenness of the sword.

90

太一在黑暗裡呈現一合相，在光明中則呈現差別相。[9]

IN darkness the One appears as uniform; in the light the One
appears as manifold.

91

大地依賴小草的幫忙，讓她看起來殷勤好客。

THE great earth makes herself hospitable with the help of the
grass.

9　「太一」（the One）可指神，造物主，或梵。落在現實面，或為了方便故，
　　或可將之想像成世間萬象。黑暗中，世間萬象的特徵隱去，看來和諧，沒
　　有分別，但在光明中，世間萬象的形象各自浮現，出現各種千差萬別的多
　　樣形貌。這裡借用佛教的「一合相」和「差別相」來譯寫前述世間萬象的
　　兩種狀態或現象。

92

樹葉生滅在漩渦的內圈，轉速急急；群星運行在漩渦較大的外圈，轉速緩緩。

THE birth and death of the leaves are the rapid whirls of the eddy whose wider circles move slowly among stars.

93

權力對世界說：「妳是我的。」

世界把權力囚禁在她的寶座上。

愛情對世界說：「我是妳的。」

世界給愛任意進出她宮室的自由。

POWER said to the world, "You are mine."

The world kept it prisoner on her throne.

Love said to the world, "I am thine."

The world gave it the freedom of her house.

94

雲霧就像大地的欲望，遮蔽了大地聲聲呼喚的太陽。[10]

THE mist is like the earth's desire. It hides the sun for whom she cries.

---

10 就佛教的觀點看，欲望是一種阻礙或障礙，這裡用雲霧作為比喻，雲霧會擋住大地的視線，使大地看不到太陽，猶如欲望之蒙蔽我們的心智。

95

靜下來，我的心！眼前的大樹正是聲聲祈禱。

BE still, my heart, these great trees are prayers.

96

剎那的喧鬧之聲竟嘲弄永恆之神的樂音。

THE noise of the moment scoffs at the music of the Eternal.

97

想到漂浮過生死以及愛欲之流的其他世代，想到那些異代群生已遭今人遺忘，一念及此，我心中於是升起了棄世的自由。

I THINK of other ages that floated upon the stream of life and love and death and are forgotten, and I feel the freedom of passing away.

98

我靈魂的憂傷是新娘的面紗；
等待入夜，有人來把面紗揭起。[11]

THE sadness of my soul is her bride's veil.
It waits to be lifted in the night.

99

死亡之印給生命之幣烙上價值，讓生命之幣得以購入真正的寶物。

DEATH'S stamp gives value to the coin of life; making it possible to buy with life what is truly precious.

---

11 這首詩與第 263 首內容一樣。

100

白雲在天之一隅謙虛靜立，
等待晨光為之加冕，敷以麗彩。

THE cloud stood humbly in a corner of the sky.
The morning crowned it with splendour.

101

塵土收下垢辱，開出鮮花朵朵作為回禮。

THE dust receives insult and in return offers her flowers.

102

別為了紀念而停下來採集花朵；你只管向前走，路上自有
鮮花不斷綻放。

DO not linger to gather flowers to keep them, but walk on, for
flowers will keep themselves blooming all your way.

103

根是樹枝，深埋土裡。
樹枝是根，挺立空中。[12]

ROOTS are the branches down in the earth.
Branches are roots in the air.

104

夏日復遼，其樂音繞著秋天飛翔，尋找舊日的巢。

THE music of the far-away summer flutters around the
Autumn seeking its former nest.

105

別自掏荷包來為朋友充場面——那是羞辱你的朋友。

DO not insult your friend by lending him merits from your
own pocket.

---

12 另一種翻譯法：根是土裡的樹枝；樹枝是空中的根。意思完全一樣，只是
　　詩的節奏不同。

106

那些無以名之的歲月的輕觸，攀附在我心頭，一如點點青苔之纏繞老樹。

THE touch of the nameless days clings to my heart like mosses round the old tree.

107

回聲模仿原音，意圖證明她自己才是本尊。

THE echo mocks her origin to prove she is the original.

108

富人一誇耀自己得到神的恩寵，神就覺得受到羞辱。

GOD is ashamed when the prosperous boasts of His special favour.

109

我自己的影子落在路的前方，因爲我有一盞燈尚未點亮。

I CAST my own shadow upon my path, because I have a lamp that has not been lighted.

110

人爲了湮滅自己心中沉默的吶喊，走入擾攘喧囂的人群。

MAN goes into the noisy crowd to drown his own clamour of silence.

111

倦怠的止盡處是死亡，完美的止盡處是無止無盡。[13]

THAT which ends in exhaustion is death, but the perfect ending is in the endless.

---

13 這首詩使用了動詞（ends），名詞（ending）和形容詞（endless）三字來構成一個巧妙的文字遊戲。翻譯理論家勒弗維爾（André Lefevere）曾提到詩裡的文字遊戲通常無法翻譯，只能想辦法補償，亦即另行創造適合譯入語語境的文字遊戲。這裡使用「止盡處」、「無止無盡」來對應，希望能保留原文的文字創意，同時傳達詩的節奏、意義與文字遊戲的趣味。

112

太陽披著素樸的光袍。雲朵盛裝打扮，穿上斑爛的彩服。

THE sun has his simple robe of light. The clouds are decked with gorgeousness.

113

群山就像孩子的聲聲吶喊，高舉手臂，想去摘星。

THE hills are like shouts of children who raise their arms, trying to catch stars.

114

行人熙攘，道路依然寂寞，因為行人不愛道路。

THE road is lonely in its crowd for it is not loved.

115

誇耀其惡行的權力被凋零的黃葉揶揄，遭飄過的白雲嘲笑。

THE power that boasts of its mischiefs is laughed at by the yellow leaves that fall, and clouds that pass by.

116

今日陽光普照，大地像個紡紗婦對我哼了一支古老的民謠，曲詞古老，如今已無人知曉。

THE earth hums to me to-day in the sun, like a woman at her spinning, some ballad of the ancient time in a forgotten tongue.

117

小草無愧於自己扎根成長的偉大世界。

THE grass-blade is worth of the great world where it grows.

118

夢是必須說話的妻子。
眠是默默受苦的丈夫。

DREAM is a wife who must talk.
Sleep is a husband who silently suffers.

119

夜吻著日漸消亡的白晝，在白晝耳邊輕聲說道：「我是死
亡，你的母親，我就來給你新的生命。」

THE night kisses the fading day whispering to his ear, "I am
death, your mother. I am to give you fresh birth."

120

暗夜啊，我能感受到妳的美——妳的美就像受寵女子熄燈
之後的樣子。

I FEEL, thy beauty, dark night, like that of the loved woman
when she has put out the lamp.

121

今生今世，我肩負著多少已逝大千世界的繁華。[14]

I CARRY in my world that flourishes the worlds that have failed.

122

親愛的朋友，多少次在暮色漸濃的黃昏，多少次在沙灘上，在濤聲裡，我感覺到你的偉大思想的寂靜。

DEAR friend, I feel the silence of your great thoughts of many a deepening eventide on this beach when I listen to these waves.

123

飛鳥認為載魚一程，讓魚飛上天空是一種善行。

THE bird thinks it is an act of kindness to give the fish a lift in the air.

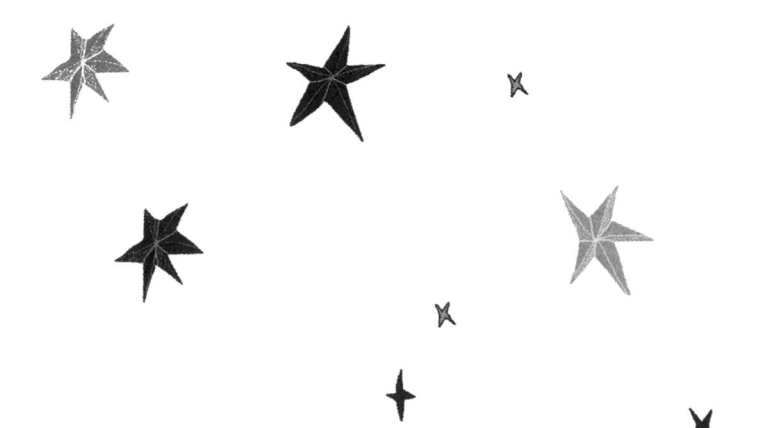

124

夜對太陽如是說：「你託月光給我捎來情書，我在草葉上給你留下含淚的答覆。」

"IN the moon thou sendest thy love letters to me, " said the night to the sun. "I leave my answers in tears upon the grass."

125

偉人是個天生的孩子，亡故後就把偉大的童年留給世人。

THE Great is a born child; when he dies he gives his great childhood to the world.

---

14 這首詩的 "my world" 與 "the worlds" 形成對照；前者是「此世」或「今世」，
　　後者是指佛教觀念裡的大千世界或「諸世」。

126

鵝卵石的完美來自流水的讚頌，並非出自鐵鎚的鑄造。

NOT hammer strokes, but dance of the water sings the pebbles into perfection.

127

蜜蜂採了蜜，離開前唱聲嗡嗡向花朵道謝。
豔麗的蝴蝶確信：理當跟他道謝的是花朵。

BEES sip honey from flowers and hum their thanks when they leave.
The gaudy butterfly is sure that the flowers owe thanks to him.

128

若你願意毫不遲疑地說出眞理，直言不諱並不難。

TO be outspoken is easy when you do not wait to speak the complete truth.

129

可能問不可能：「你的居所何在？」
不可能答道：「無能者的夢裡。」

ASKS the Possible to the Impossible, "Where is your dwelling place?"
"In the dreams of the impotent," comes the answer.

130

假如你把所有錯誤都擋在門外，眞理亦不得其門而入。

IF you shut your door to all errors truth will be shut out.

131

在憂傷的心的後面，我聽見一陣窸窸窣窣的聲響——我看不見那聲響來自何處。

I HEAR some rustle of things behind my sadness of heart, — I cannot see them.

132

活動之中的休閒是工作。
大海的寧靜湧動於波濤之中。

LEISURE in its activity is work.
The stillness of the sea stirs in waves.

133

葉子有愛化成花，
花朵有敬變成果。

THE leaf becomes flower when it loves.
The flower becomes fruit when it worships.

134

地裡的根讓樹枝結出果實纍纍，不求回報。

THE roots below the earth claim no rewards for making the
branches fruitful.

135

落雨的黃昏，風吹個不停。

我望著飄搖的枝葉，琢磨著萬物的偉大。

THIS rainy evening the wind is restless.

I look at the swaying branches and ponder over the greatness of all things.

136

午夜的暴風雨像太早醒過來的大孩子，逕自開始玩樂，大聲叫嚷。

STORM of midnight, like a giant child awakened in the untimely dark, has begun to play and shout.

137

啊大海，妳這遭受暴風雨遺棄的新娘，妳掀起波濤滾滾，
終究還是追不上妳的情郎。

THOU raisest thy waves vainly to follow thy lover. O sea,
thou lonely bride of the storm.

138

文字對作品說：「我如此空洞，真是慚愧。」
作品對文字說：「看到你，我才發現我的貧瘠。」[15]

"I AM ashamed of my emptiness," said the Word to the Work.
"I know how poor I am when I see you," said the Work to the
Word.

---

15 原文把 "Word" 和 "Work" 擬人化，使之互相對話；兩字都用大寫，因此中
   文以粗體字表示，分別譯為「文字」與「作品」。這是筆者的解讀。另外
   由於泰戈爾對《聖經》也有所了解，所以這裡的 "Word" 也可以譯為「道」，
   如此，與之相對（又相輔相成）的 "Work" 就可譯為「事工」或「德行」。

139

時間是變化的財富，但時鐘只是時間的諧擬，因而只有變化，沒有財富。

TIME is the wealth of change, but the clock in its parody makes it mere change and no wealth.

140

眞理穿上連身裙，發現事實過於拘束；
換上虛構的大衣，眞理終於行動自如。

TRUTH in her dress finds facts too tight.
In fiction she moves with ease.

141

路啊，從前浪跡東西的我討厭過你；但是你已帶領我走遍天涯海角，我如今已無法離開你，與你在愛裡合一。

WHEN I travelled to here and to there, I was tired of thee, O Road, but now when thou leadest me to everywhere I am wedded to thee in love.

142

就讓我這麼想吧：繁星之中，必定有那麼一顆會指引我，
帶領我走過未知的黑暗。

LET me think that there is one among those stars that guides
my life through the dark unknown.

143

女人啊，經妳纖指一點撥，我的器物出現了秩序，宛如樂
音響起。

WOMAN, with the grace of your fingers you touched my
things and order came out like music.

144

有一悲傷的聲音築巢在歲月的廢墟。

夜裡，這聲音對我歌唱：「我愛過你。」

ONE sad voice has its nest among the ruins of the years.
It sings to me in the night, — "I loved you."

145

燃燒中的火焰以自身的光芒對我示警，要我切勿靠近。

這警示救了我，讓我遠離掩藏在灰下的餘燼。

THE flaming fire warns me off by its own glow.
Save me from the dying embers hidden under ashes.

146

儘管屋內那盞小燈尚未點亮，

但是我有繁星點點，閃爍在天。

I HAVE my stars in the sky,
But oh for my little lamp unlit in my house.

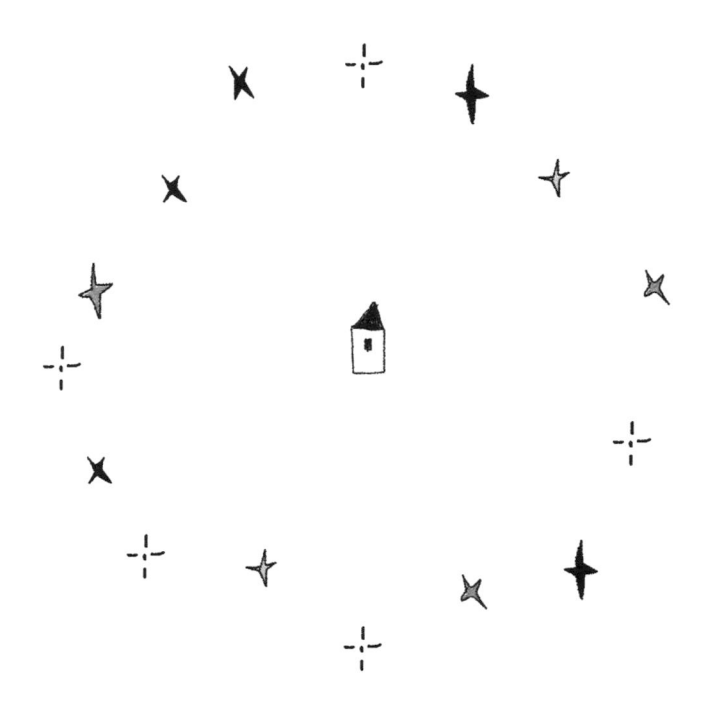

147

死去的文字之塵緊緊黏著你；
請用沉默洗淨你的靈魂。

THE dust of the dead words clings to thee.
Wash thy soul with silence.

148

生命裡有許多裂隙，死亡的哀音從中流瀉而出。

GAPS are left in life through which comes the sad music of death.

149

一早，世界就打開光明之心。
我的心，出來吧！帶著愛來與世界相見。

THE world has opened its heart of light in the morning.
Come out, my heart, with thy love to meet it.

150

我的思緒隨著微微閃爍的葉子而閃爍，我的心隨著陽光的撫觸歌唱；此生我樂於與萬物同浮沉——浮上空間的湛藍，沉入時間的黯黝。

MY thoughts shimmer with these shimmering leaves and my heart sings with the touch of this sunlight; my life is glad to be floating with all things into the blue of space, into the dark of time.

151

神的超凡力量見於輕拂的微風，不見於狂風暴雨。

GOD'S great power is in the gentle breeze, not in the storm.

152

夢裡，萬物亂了序，壓迫著我；醒來，我將發現萬物在祢那裡歸隊，我也將獲得自由。

THIS is a dream in which things are all loose and they oppress. I shall find them gathered in thee when I awake and shall be free.

153

落日問：「誰來接手我的任務？」
陶燈答：「主人，我會盡力而為。」

"WHO is there to take up my duties?" asked the setting sun.
"I shall do what I can, my Master," said the earthen lamp.

154

摘下花瓣，你可收集不到花的美麗。

BY plucking her petals you do not gather the beauty of the flower.

155

沉默會護持你的聲音，猶如鳥巢保護睡鳥。

SILENCE will carry your voice like the nest that holds the sleeping birds.

156

偉人與倭儒並肩，胸懷坦蕩；
凡夫遇見倭儒，刻意保持疏離。

THE Great walks with the Small without fear.
The Middling keeps aloof.

157

夜悄悄開出朵朵鮮花，讓白晝領受所有的恩謝。

THE night opens the flowers in secret and allows the day to get thanks.

158

受害者的苦苦掙扎，當權者視之為忘恩負義。

POWER takes as ingratitude the writhings of its victims.

159

如果能在圓滿中歡慶，我們就能與果實欣然告別。

WHEN we rejoice in our fulness, then we can part with our fruits with joy.

160

雨點吻著大地，悄聲說道：「母親啊，我們是想家的孩子，我們從天上回到妳懷裡了。」

THE raindrops kissed the earth and whispered, — "We are thy homesick children, mother, come back to thee from the heaven."

161

蛛網佯裝要網住露珠，結果網住的是蒼蠅。

THE cobweb pretends to catch dew-drops and catches flies.

162

愛情啊！你走來，手持令人痛苦的熾熱燈火；我看見你的臉，認得你是天賜至福。

LOVE! when you come with the burning lamp of pain in your hand, I can see your face and know you as bliss.

163

螢火蟲對星星說：「智者說你們的光總有一天會熄滅。」
星星聽了，甚麼話也沒說。

"THE learned say that your lights will one day be no more."
said the firefly to the stars.
The stars made no answer.

164

暮色蒼茫，一隻黎明之鳥飛入我沉默的巢。

IN the dusk of the evening the bird of some early dawn comes
to the nest of my silence.

165

思緒紛飛，就像空中飛過的雁群。
我聽見他們振翼翱翔的聲音。

THOUGHTS pass in my mind like flocks of ducks in the sky.
I hear the voice of their wings.

166

運河就愛這麼想：河川存在的唯一理由就是給運河供水。

THE canal loves to think that rivers exist solely to supply it
with water.

167

世界以其痛苦親吻我的靈魂，要我詠歌作為回報。

THE world has kissed my soul with its pain, asking for its
return in songs.

168

壓迫著我的，是我那嘗試出走的靈魂？還是世界的靈魂正
在輕叩我心，要求進門？

THAT which oppresses me, is it my soul trying to come out in
the open, or the soul of the world knocking at my heart for its
entrance?

169

思想從自己的語言文字獲得滋養，日漸成長。

THOUGHT feeds itself with its own words and grows.

170

我把心靈之瓶浸入這寧靜時刻，汲滿了整整一瓶的愛。

I HAVE dipped the vessel of my heart into this silent hour; it has filled with love.

171

要嘛你有事可忙，要嘛你無所事事。

一旦你不得不說：「讓我們做點事吧！」胡鬧就從這裡開始。

EITHER you have work or you have not.
When you have to say, "Let us do something," then begins mischief.

172

太陽花羞於承認無名小花是她的親戚。

太陽東升，笑問那無名小花：「親愛的，妳還好嗎？」[16]

THE sunflower blushed to own the nameless flower as her kin.
The sun rose and smiled on it, saying, "Are you well, my darling? "

173

「是誰像命運那樣逼著我向前奔走？」

「是跨騎在我背上的**自我**。」 [17]

"WHO drives me forward like fate?"

"The Myself striding on my back."

174

雲注滿了河川的水杯，紛紛躲入遙遠的群山背後。

THE clouds fill the watercups of the river, hiding themselves in the distant hills.

---

16 這裡的「太陽花」（sunflower）固然可以譯成「向日葵」，但是為了和下一句的「太陽」（the sun）作對照，這裡選譯為「太陽花」。兩者名相雖然接近，心胸畢竟不同。

17 此詩第二句中的「自我」（myself），英文用的是大寫：Myself，中文並無大小寫之分，因而「自我」以粗體字表示。

175

回家途中，我潑灑著罐中之水；
待我返家，罐中之水已經所剩無幾。

I SPILL water from my water jar as I walk on my way,
Very little remains for my home.

176

瓶中之水瀏亮，海中之水黝暗。
淺近之道的文字清晰；深奧的眞理肅穆無語。[18]

THE water in a vessel is sparkling; the water in the sea is
dark.
The small truth has words that are clear; the great truth has
great silence.

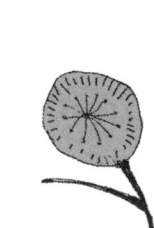

177

你的笑容是你自己田裡的花朵，你的談話是你自己山上的松濤，但你的心卻是我們都認識的那位女子。

YOUR smile was the flowers of your own fields, your talk was the rustle of your own mountain pines, but your heart was the woman that we all know.

178

尋常小物，我留給摯愛；偉大器物，我留給眾生。

IT is the little things that I leave behind for my loved ones, — great things are for everyone.

---

18 這首哲理詩的第一行是個引子，以瓶中之水與海中之水說明深淺的差別，第二句再點明道理有淺近與深奧之分。文字是道理的載具，淺近的道理，文字的載具猶可一用，深奧的道理因為十分複雜，文字的載具就無法予以全部承載，此詩詩意十分接近老子的「大音希聲，大象無形」。

179

女人，妳以豐沛的淚水環抱世界之心，就像大海環抱著陸地。

WOMAN, thou hast encircled the world's heart with the depth of thy tears as the sea has the earth.

180

陽光以微笑跟我打招呼，他憂傷的妹妹——細雨，則來跟我談心。

THE sunshine greets me with a smile. The rain, his sad sister, talks to my heart.

181

我的白晝之花落下片片花瓣，遺忘一旁。
這朵花在黃昏成熟，結出記憶的金果。

MY flower of the day dropped its petals forgotten.
In the evening it ripens into a golden fruit of memory.

182

我像夜裡的道路，靜靜聆聽記憶的跫音。

I AM like the road in the night listening to the footfalls of its memories in silence.

183

對我而言，黃昏的天空像一扇窗，窗內亮著一盞燈，還有一個等待的人。

THE evening sky to me is like a window, and a lighted lamp, and a waiting behind it.

184

人若過分忙於行善，就沒有時間做個好人。

HE who is too busy doing good finds no time to be good.

185

我是雨水落盡的秋雲，要尋找我的豐盈，去看成熟的稻田。[19]

I AM the autumn cloud, empty of rain, see my fulness in the field of ripened rice.

186

他們恨，他們殺，他們得到人們的頌讚。
可神覺得羞愧，忙著把祂那些記憶往青草地裡埋。

THEY hated and killed and men praised them.
But God in shame hastens to hide its memory under the green grass.

187

腳趾是已經拋棄了自己過去的手指。

TOES are the fingers that have forsaken their past.

188

黑暗走向光明，目盲走向死亡。

DARKNESS travels towards light, but blindness towards death.

189

寵物狗懷疑：宇宙正在密謀掠奪牠的地盤。

THE pet dog suspects the universe for scheming to take its place.

---

19 泰戈爾的詩看似簡單，其實很重視用字、節奏與格律。就格律來說，我們極少在此集子裡看到我們習見的尾韻，倒是頭韻十分常見，例如這首詩的第二句就用了兩個頭韻（alliteration）："fulness"與"field"兩字押了 /f/ 頭韻，"ripened"與"rice"押了 /r/ 的頭韻。頭韻或可類比為中文的雙聲詞，如「瀰漫」，「琵琶」等語詞。不過中文雙聲詞量並不多，歷來也不是詩法正宗，因而極難找到聲母剛好一樣的語詞來對譯頭韻。翻譯理論家勒弗維爾建議另行創造或改用其他適合譯入語的用韻方式，這裡改以類似尾韻的「秋雲」與「豐盈」作為翻譯補償。

190

靜靜坐好，我的心，別揚起塵埃。

讓世界自己找到路，走到你身旁。

SIT still my heart, do not raise your dust.
Let the world find its way to you.

191

發射前，彎弓悄聲對箭矢說：「你的自由是我的自由。」

THE bow whispers to the arrow before it speeds forth — "Your
freedom is mine."

192

女人，妳的笑聲藏著生命之泉的樂音。

WOMAN, in your laughter you have the music of the fountain
of life.

193

僅有理智的心，猶如有刃無柄的刀，
只會讓使用者的手鮮血直流。

A MIND all logic is like a knife all blade.
It makes the hand bleed that uses it.

194

神愛戀人間的燈火，更甚於自己偉大的星辰。

GOD loves man's lamp lights better than his own great stars.

195

這世界原本狂暴，一經美麗的樂音調伏，今日終於無雨也
無風。

THIS world is the world of wild storms kept tame with the
music of beauty.

196

晚霞對太陽如是說：「我的心像個金盒，滿滿都是你的吻。」

"MY heart is like the golden casket of thy kiss," said the sunset cloud to the sun.

197

親近，你可能施加傷害；遠離，你或能得到所愛。

BY touching you may kill, by keeping away you may possess.

198

蟋蟀唧唧，細雨淅瀝，在暗夜裡一起朝我走來，猶如夢的沙沙聲，來自我遠逝的青春。

THE cricket's chirp and the patter of rain come to me through the dark, like the rustle of dreams from my past youth.

199

小花向剛剛失去滿天星斗的晨空哭訴：「我失去了我的露珠。」[20]

"I HAVE lost my dewdrop," cries the flower to the morning sky that has lost all its stars.

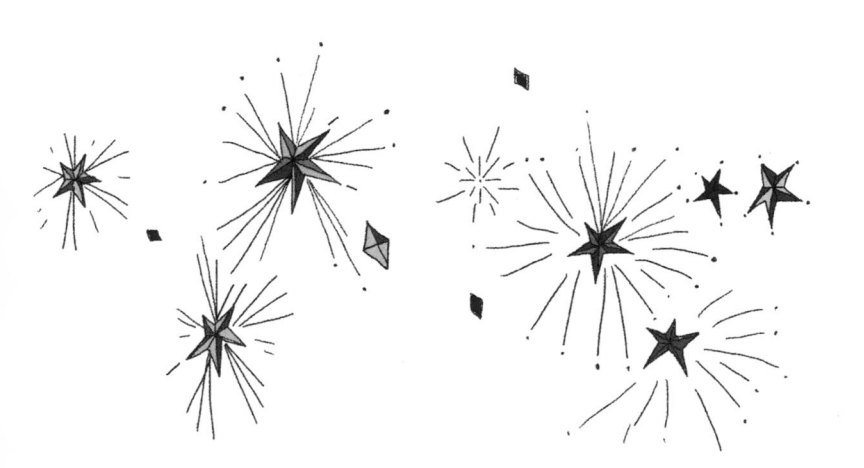

---

20 這首詩描寫了晨空、星星、小花、露珠在太陽出來之後的變化或際遇：太陽一出，露珠蒸發，星斗隱退。除此之外，詩人也同時藉對話與擬人化的手法，展現「大失」與「小虧」的對比：晨空失去了所有星星（all its stars），小花失去了她的露珠——從英文的 "I have lost my dewdrop" 看來，小花只有一顆露珠而已。不過，小花顯然很寶貝她的露珠，因而哭著跟晨空抱怨。這聲抱怨除了可愛，也十分有趣；這趣味寓於小花的不知其失之小，也不知其抱怨對象的「失」有多大。藉此，詩人的哲思呼之欲出：大小是個相對的概念，從心而觀，或許無所謂大，也無所謂小，是大是小，存乎一心而已。

200

焚燒的木頭渾身冒出火焰，大聲叫道：「這是我的花朵，
我的死亡。」

THE burning log bursts in flame and cries, — "This is my
flower, my death."

201

黃蜂認為蜜蜂鄰居的蜂房過於狹小，
哪知道這位鄰居反倒拜託他蓋個更小的。[21]

THE wasp thinks that the honey-hive of the neighbouring
bees
is too small.
His neighbours ask him to build one still smaller.

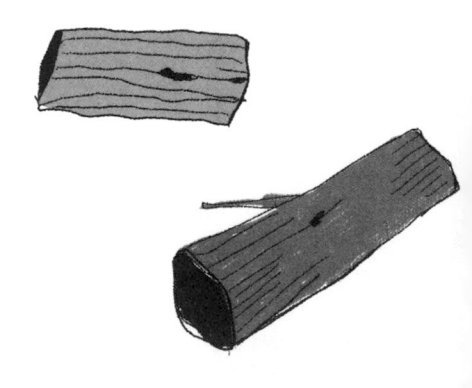

202

河岸對河流說：「我留不住你的波浪，
且讓我在心裡留下你的足跡。」

"I CANNOT keep your waves," says the bank to the river.
"Let me keep your footprints in my heart."

203

白晝以這小小世界的喧囂，淹沒所有大千世界的寂靜。

THE day, with the noise of this little earth, drowns the silence
of all worlds.

---

21 這首詩與第 199 首的主題頗為相似，亦即所謂大或所謂小，端看使用者如
何看待而已；換言之，大小並非絕對，而是相對的。

204

歌唱頌天空的無限，畫描繪大地的廣袤，詩吟詠天空與大地的遼闊；

因爲詩的文字有意義可行走於大地，有音韻可飛翔在天空。

THE song feels the infinite in the air, the picture in the earth,
the poem in the air and the earth;
For its words have meaning that walks and music that soars.

205

當太陽落入西山，東方的淸晨早已默默佇立在太陽的前方。

WHEN the sun goes down to the West, the East of his
morning stands before him in silence.

206

別讓我在這世上站錯位置，教這世界與我爲敵。

LET me not put myself wrongly to my world and set it against me.

207

讚美讓我羞愧，只因我曾暗地裡乞求讚美。

PRAISE shames me, for I secretly beg for it.

208

無事可做時，就讓我無所事事吧！讓我安然處在無所事事的寧靜深處，猶如大海靜下來的濱海黃昏。

LET my doing nothing when I have nothing to do become untroubled in its depth of peace like the evening in the seashore when the water is silent.

209

啊少女，妳的清純宛如湖水的湛藍，展現妳眞實的深度。

MAIDEN, your simplicity, like the blueness of the lake, reveals your depth of truth.

210

完美並不孤行，身邊總有衆緣相隨。

THE best does not come alone. It comes with the company of the all.

211

神的右手溫柔，左手可怖。

GOD's right hand is gentle, but terrible is his left hand.

212

我的黃昏從陌生的林子裡走來，說著晨星聽不懂的語言。

MY evening came among the alien trees and spoke in a
language which my morning stars did not know.

213

夜的魆黑是個袋子，滿滿裝著黎明的金光。

NIGHT'S darkness is a bag that bursts with the gold of the
dawn.

214

我們的欲望給如雲似霧的人生增添一抹彩虹的顏色。

OUR desire lends the colours of the rainbow to the mere mists
and vapours of life.

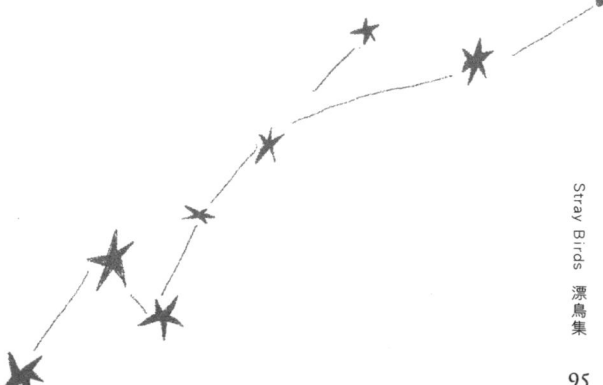

215

神等著從世人手中贏回一份禮物——當初祂贈與世人的鮮花。

GOD waits to win back his own flowers as gifts from man's hands.

216

我的憂思戲弄我，問我他們可有名姓。

MY sad thoughts tease me asking me their own names.

217

果實的供獻很珍稀，花朵的供獻很甜蜜，但是讓我的供獻如同樹葉，謙恭地默默地垂下綠蔭。

THE service of the fruit is precious, the service of the flower is sweet, but let my service be the service of the leaves in its shade of humble devotion.

218

我心揚帆，迎著慵懶的風，航向天涯海角的夢幻島。

MY heart has spread its sails to the idle winds for the shadowy island of Anywhere.

219

群眾殘酷，人類善良。

MEN are cruel, but Man is kind.

220

讓我化作你的酒杯，把我的盈滿獻給你和你的摯愛。

MAKE me thy cup and let my fullness be for thee and for thine.

221

暴風雨像某位天神的痛哭，因爲他的愛被大地回絕。

THE storm is like the cry of some god in pain whose love the earth refuses.

222

世界圓滿不漏，因爲死亡不是一道裂隙。

THE world does not leak because death is not a crack.

223

生命因錯過的愛，變得更加豐富。

LIFE has become richer by the love that has been lost.

224

朋友，你偉大的心散發著朝陽的光芒，有如黎明時分覆雪的孤山頂峰。

MY friend, your great heart shone with the sunrise of the East like the snowy summit of a lonely hill in the dawn.

225

死亡的噴泉，讓生命的止水噴出水花。

THE fountain of death makes the still water of life play.

226

神啊，那些擁有一切但不信神的人，嘲笑那些一無所有但信神的人。

THOSE who have everything but thee, my God, laugh at those who have nothing but thyself.

227

生命的律動在自己的音樂裡找到安頓之處。

THE movement of life has its rest in its own music.

228

踢，只能踢起塵土，踢不出地裡的作物。[22]

KICKS only raise dust and not crops from the earth.

229

我們的名字是夜裡海上的波光，**轉瞬即逝**，不留痕跡。

OUR names are the light that glows on the sea waves at night and then dies without leaving its signature.

230

讓有眼光看見玫瑰的人，只看見花梗上密密的刺。

LET him only see the thorns who has eyes to see the rose.

---

22 這首詩的趣味在於用字。英語動詞 "raise" 具有多重意義，要確切把握其詞意，必須看後面的受詞來決定。在這裡，這個動詞分別帶領兩個受詞，一是「塵土」（dust），一是「作物」（crops），意謂「踢」（kicks）這些動作，僅能「raise 起塵土」，「raise 不起作物」。中文翻譯可能無法如實複製 "raise" 這個字在這裡的多義性，因此這裡採用語詞轉化（conversion）與增譯（amplification）的技巧，將焦點擺在 "kicks" 這個字上，另行創譯一個適合入譯入語語境的文字遊戲。

231

雙翼鑲金的鳥，再也無法翱翔天際。

SET bird's wings with gold and it will never again soar in the sky.

232

家鄉的蓮花綻放在這異域的水上；一樣的蓮花，一樣的香氣，只是換了另一個名字。[23]

THE same lotus of our clime blooms here in the alien water with the same sweetness, under another name.

233

由心觀之，隔閡令人生畏。

IN heart's perspective the distance looms large.

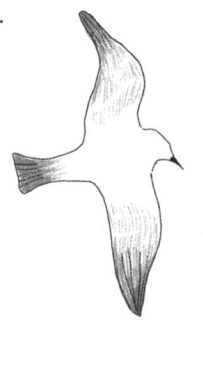

234

月亮把清輝灑向夜空，把暗色的斑點留給她自己。

THE moon has her light all over the sky, her dark spots to herself.

235

別說：「這是早晨。」隨即以昨日之名將之拋棄。你應該看著早晨，猶如生平首見，猶如看見尚未命名的初生嬰兒。

DO not say, "It is morning," and dismiss it with a name of yesterday. See it for the first time as a new-born child that has no name.

---

23 莎士比亞筆下的茱麗葉也說過相似的話："What's in a name? that which we call a rose / By any other name would smell as sweet."（*Romeo and Juliet*, Act 2, Scene 2），亦即名字／名相算甚麼呢？玫瑰這種花，如果我們不叫她「玫瑰」，她的香味還是一樣甜美。泰戈爾在這裡似乎呼應了茱麗葉的提問，點出家鄉的蓮花即使移植異地，換了名字，不論花相還是花香還是依然如故。這比茱麗葉或莎士比亞更進一步肯定了名相的不足為憑。這首詩放在全球化如火如荼的二十一世紀來閱讀，除了有古今中西互文的趣味之外，對於飄零四海的離散心靈而言，更是別有一番滋味在心頭。

236

煙向天空誇耀，灰向大地吹噓，兩個都說自己是火的兄弟。

SMOKE boasts to the sky, and Ashes to the earth, that they are
brothers to the fire.

237

雨點悄聲對茉莉花說：「永遠把我留在你心裡。」
茉莉花「唉」了一聲，凋落在地。[24]

THE raindrop whispered to the jasmine, "Keep me in your
heart for ever."
The jasmine sighed, "Alas," and dropped to the ground.

238

羞怯的思緒啊，別害怕。
我是個詩人。

TIMID thoughts, do not be afraid of me.
I am a poet.

239

我心中朦朧的寧靜似乎充滿了蟋蟀的唧唧——那是聲音的
灰色曙光。

THE dim silence of my mind seems filled with crickets' chirp
— the grey twilight of sound.

---

24 這首詩描繪的既是雨中小景，也是一幕可愛的短劇。要了解這首詩的趣味，
大概首先要了解茉莉花這種植物的特性（不然讀完就會摸不著頭緒）。放
在印度的語境，這裡的茉莉花有可能是雙瓣茉莉（*Jasminum sambac*）；無論
如何，茉莉這種花本來生性脆弱，風一吹，雨一打就馬上掉落。在這首詩
裡，詩人為雨打花落這幕雨中即景構思了一段愛的短劇：雨點愛上茉莉花，
投入茉莉花的花心，希望茉莉花永遠把他放在心上，奈何茉莉花的「心」
本來就放不下任何他者，不論有形（雨）無形（風）都一樣。結局當然是
茉莉花嘆了一聲，頹然落地。這首詩可與第 197 首合而觀之，即「親近，
你可能施加傷害；遠離，你或能得到所愛。」

240

爆竹啊，你向群星挑戰，你的無禮尾隨著你，重又回歸大地。[25]

ROCKETS, your insult to the stars follows yourself back to the earth.

241

你已經引領我穿過白晝的喧嘩，走入黃昏的孤寂。
我守在長夜的寧靜裡，等候這段歷程的意義。

THOU hast led me through my crowded travels of the day to my evening's loneliness.
I wait for its meaning through the stillness of the night.

242

此生猶如橫渡大海，我們在同一艘狹窄的船上相遇。
在死亡中，我們抵達彼岸，各自奔向不同的下一站。

THIS life is the crossing of a sea, where we meet in the same narrow ship.
In death we reach the shore and go to our different worlds.

243

眞理的河川不知流經多少錯誤的支流。

THE stream of truth flows through its channels of mistakes.

244

今日我的心充滿鄉愁，想念時間之海彼端的那一刻甜蜜時光。

MY heart is homesick to-day for the one sweet hour across the sea of time.

---

25 英文字 "rocket" 可以是火箭，也可以是爆竹。翻譯是一段選擇的過程，圖里（Gideon Toury）等二十世紀翻譯理論學者認為，這種選擇應考慮譯入語文化的規範等等因素；這裡選用「爆竹」是基於文化以及時代的考量。

245

嗍啾的鳥鳴是晨光重返大地的回聲。

THE bird-song is the echo of the morning light back from the earth.

246

晨光問金鳳花：「你就這麼驕傲，連親都不肯親我一下？」[26]

"ARE you too proud to kiss me?" the morning light asks the buttercup.

247

小花問：「啊太陽，我該如何歌唱，如何對你禮敬？」太陽答：「以你素樸寧靜的純潔。」

"HOW may I sing to thee and worship, O Sun?" asked the little flower. "By the simple silence of thy purity," answered the sun.

248

人一旦變成禽獸，就禽獸不如。

MAN is worse than an animal when he is an animal.

249

陽光一吻，烏雲瞬間化為天堂繁花。

DARK clouds become heaven's flowers when kissed by light.

---

26 這首詩與第 237 首相似，即詩的發想都是從描寫對象的特性入手。金鳳花（buttercup）是一種長在路邊或野地裡的黃色小花，單瓣五瓣，形狀如杯，早年又譯杯狀花。這花可能和牽牛花類似，太陽一出來就會枯萎。詩中的晨光不知金鳳花的這一特性，只知他一出現，金鳳花就垂下臉龐，因此心生懷疑，以為金鳳花是因為太傲慢，不肯與他親近。詩人超絕的想像力，把一個單純的自然現象化為一幕可愛的戲劇，有愛慕，有誤會，充滿了張力。

250

莫讓劍刃嘲笑劍柄的鈍。

LET not the sword-blade mock its handle for being blunt.

251

夜的寧靜，像一盞長燈，幽幽亮著銀河的光。

THE night's silence, like a deep lamp, is burning with the light of its milky way.

252

環繞著陽光燦爛的生命之島，大海日夜高唱著死亡之歌，無止，無休。

AROUND the sunny island of Life swells day and night death's limitless song of the sea.

253

這山不就像一朵花嗎？山丘開展，恰似正在啜飲陽光的片片花瓣。

IS not this mountain like a flower, with its petals of hills, drinking the sunlight?

254

如果誤讀眞實的意義，顚倒其重點，眞實就不成其爲眞實。[27]

THE real with its meaning read wrong and emphasis misplaced is the unreal.

---

27 這首詩的重點是「眞實」（the real）和「非眞實」（the unreal）的對照。中文無法在單字前面加個前綴（prefix）來改變詞意，因此這裡從反方向著手，以半帶解釋的方式對譯。當然若是其他非詩的文類，或許這種狀況就可以附上原文，譯成「如果誤讀眞實（the real）的意義，顚倒其重點，眞實就成為非眞實（the unreal）」。

255

我的心啊，從世間的運行之中尋找你的美，恰似小舟得到風的吹送，水之推波。

FIND your beauty, my heart, from the world's movement, like the boat that has the grace of the wind and the water.

256

眼睛不以自己的眼界為傲，倒以眼鏡自豪。

THE eyes are not proud of their sight but of their eyeglasses.

257

我生活在小小的世界，深怕這小小的世界越變越小。
請拔舉我到你的世界！讓我享有樂於放棄一切的自由。

I LIVE in this little world of mine and am afraid to make it the least less.
Lift me into thy world and let me have the freedom gladly to lose my all.

258

虛假終究無法憑靠權力的增長，逐漸變成眞知灼見。[28]

THE false can never grow into truth by growing in power.

259

我的心渴望以歌的盪漾清波，輕輕撫觸這陽光燦爛的綠色世界。

MY heart, with its lapping waves of song, longs to caress this green world of the sunny day.

---

28 英文動詞 "grow" 有多重意義，端看後面接的受詞之性質如何，如與「小孩」連在一起，其意為「成長」，若與「事業」連在一起，其意為「發展」等。這裡連接了「真理」（truth）與「權力」（power），因為語言使用的限制，中文翻譯使用了「變成」與「增長」兩個動詞來對譯，多少損失了 "grow" 的多義性。

260

路邊草，愛那星子吧！你的夢就會在繁花之中一一綻放。

WAYSIDE grass, love the star, then your dreams will come out in flowers.

261

願你的樂音如劍，直刺市井喧囂的中心。

LET your music, like a sword, pierce the noise of the market to its heart.

262

這一樹顫動的葉，就像嬰兒的手指，輕輕碰觸著我的心。

THE trembling leaves of this tree touch my heart like the fingers of an infant child.

263

我靈魂的憂傷是新娘的面紗；

等待入夜，有人來把面紗揭起。[29]

THIS sadness of my soul is her bride's veil.

It waits to be lifted in the night.

264

小花如今躺在塵土裡；

她尋覓過蝴蝶的小徑。[30]

THE little flower lies in the dust.

It sought the path of the butterfly.

---

29 這首詩與第 98 首重複，坊間許多版本刪去這一首，這裡予以保留。

30 欲了解這首詩的趣味與動人處，關鍵是要注意上下兩句英文時態的變化。
第一句 "The little flower lies in the dust" 描寫小花躺在塵土裡，動詞 "lies" 是
現在式，第三人稱單數，說明小花「此時此刻／一向如此」的狀態。當然
我們知道小花不是一直都躺在塵土裡，因此詩人在第二句他超人的想像
力與同情心給了我們一個解釋：原來小花是因為之前追尋蝴蝶飛過的空中
小徑（It sought the path of the butterfly），此時此刻才會掉落在塵土裡。注
意這一句的動詞是「尋找過／找過」（"sought"）。若保持與第一句同樣的
第三人稱單數現在式，則應用 "seeks"，而非 "sought"。若第二句是用 "seeks"，
則全詩純粹只是自然景物的描寫，改成過去式 "sought"，整首詩的意境全
然改觀，讀者彷彿可以看見一齣美麗淒婉的追尋故事正在眼前上演，而小
花此刻躺在塵土裡的形象令人頓時覺得十分同情。

265

我在路的世界裡行走。夜幕降臨，家的天地啊，請打開你的大門。

I AM in the world of the roads. The night comes. Open thy gate, thou world of the home.

266

白晝之歌我已唱完。天色已晚，讓我打起燈籠，走過驟雨飄風的小路。

I HAVE sung the songs of thy day. In the evening let me carry thy lamp through the stormy path.

267

我不要你進入我的住屋；
我的情人，我要你走入我無盡的寂寞。

I DO not ask thee into the house.
Come into my infinite loneliness, my Lover.

268

死亡屬於人生，誕生也是；舉步是行走，落腳也是。

DEATH belongs to life as birth does. The walk is in the raising
of the foot as in the laying of it down.

269

你在繁花與陽光之中留下的素樸細語，其意義我已明瞭；
請教導我，讓我了解那些關於痛苦和死亡的話語。

I HAVE learnt the simple meaning of thy whispers in flowers
and sunshine — teach me to know thy words in pain and
death.

270

晨光一吻,遲到的暗夜之花打了個寒顫,嘆息一聲,凋落在地。

THE night's flower was late when the morning kissed her, she shivered and sighed and dropped to the ground.

271

在萬物的悲哀裡,我聽見永恆之母的低吟。

THROUGH the sadness of all things I hear the crooning of the Eternal Mother.

272

大地啊，來到你岸邊的那時我是個陌生人，住進你屋裡的
那時我是個賓客，離開你家門的今日，我已成爲你的友人。

I CAME to your shore as a stranger, I lived in your house as a
guest, I leave your door as a friend, my earth.

273

我走後，讓我的思念來陪伴你，猶如一抹落日餘暉，依偎
在靜默的星空邊緣。

LET my thoughts come to you, when I am gone, like the
afterglow of sunset at the margin of starry silence.

274

在我心中點亮休憩的黃昏星，讓黑夜在我耳邊悄聲傾訴愛的細語。

LIGHT in my heart the evening star of rest and then let the night whisper to me of love.

275

我是走在黑暗中的小孩。

母親，我伸出雙手，穿過夜幕來把妳尋找。

I AM a child in the dark.
I stretch my hands through the coverlet of night for thee, Mother.

276

日間的工作已經結束。母親，把我的臉藏在妳的臂彎。讓我進入夢鄉。

THE day of work is done. Hide my face in your arms, Mother. Let me dream.

277

相聚時，燈火長明；離別之際，燈火轉瞬熄滅。

THE lamp of meeting burns long; it goes out in a moment at the parting.

278

世界啊，我死後，請在你的靜默中爲我留下一句話：「我曾愛過。」

ONE word keep for me in thy silence, O World, when I am dead, "I have loved."

279

只有愛這個世界，我們才算活在世上。

WE live in this world when we love it.

280

讓死者享有不朽的令譽，讓生者享有不朽的愛情。

LET the dead have the immortality of fame, but the living the immortality of love.

281

我曾見過祢：就像個半夢半醒的小孩在黎明的微光中看見母親，我就那麼微微一笑，再次進入夢鄉。

I HAVE seen thee as the half-awakened child sees his mother in the dusk of the dawn and then smiles and sleeps again.

282

爲了解生命的永無止盡，我將一而再，再而三地死了又死。

I SHALL die again and again to know that life is inexhaustible.

283

我和眾人在路上行走，看見你站在陽台上微笑，我便引吭高歌，忘掉所有喧囂。

WHILE I was passing with the crowd in the road I saw thy smile from the balcony and I sang and forgot all noise.

284

愛是完滿充實的生命，宛如斟滿的酒杯。

LOVE is life in its fullness like the cup with its wine.

285

他們點燃自己的燈火，吟唱自己的歌，聚集在自己的神殿裡。

但是群鳥歌唱祢的名，沐浴著祢的晨曦——因爲祢的名字是喜悅。

THEY light their own lamps and sing their own words in their temples.
But the birds sing thy name in thine own morning light, — for thy name is joy.

286

引領我到祢靜默的深處，讓頌歌充滿我心。

LEAD me in the centre of thy silence to fill my heart with songs.

287

就讓他們住在煙火嘶嘶的世間吧，那是他們的選擇。
神啊，我的心渴慕祢的繁星點點。

LET them live who choose in their own hissing world of
fireworks.
My heart longs for thy stars, my God.

288

愛的痛苦繞著我的生命高歌，有如深不可測的大海；愛的
喜悅有如群鳥，聚在繁花盛開的林中歡唱。

LOVE'S pain sang round my life like the unplumbed sea, and
love's joy sang like birds in its flowering groves.

289

你想熄燈，那就熄吧。
我願意認識你的黑暗，愛上你的黑暗。

PUT out the lamp when thou wishest.
I shall know thy darkness and shall love it.

290

白日的盡頭處，我站在你面前；你將看到我的傷疤，知道我曾受傷，也知道我已痊癒。

WHEN I stand before thee at the day's end thou shalt see my scars and know that I had my wounds and also my healing.

291

有朝一日，我將在另一個世界的日出時分對祢歌唱：「我曾見過祢，在大地的亮光之中，在世人的愛裡。」

SOME day I shall sing to thee in the sunrise of some other world, "I have seen thee before in the light of the earth, n the love of man."

292

昔日的浮雲飄入我生命，不再颶風，不再下雨，只爲我帶來一抹色彩，點染黃昏的天空。

CLOUDS come floating into my life from other days no longer to shed rain or usher storm but to give colour to my sunset sky.

293

真理揚起反抗自身的風暴，讓風暴散播自己的種子。

TRUTH raises against itself the storm that scatters its seeds broadcast.

294

昨夜的風雨爲今日的清晨加冕，冠之以金色的和平。

THE storm of the last night has crowned this morning with golden peace.

295

眞理似乎帶著結論而來；這結論又催生下一個結論。

TRUTH seems to come with its final word; and the final word gives birth to its next.

296

有福之人，名實相符。

BLESSED is he whose fame does not outshine his truth.

297

一旦我忘記自己的名字，你甜蜜的名字就充滿我心，宛如雲霧散盡，朝陽冉冉升起。

SWEETNESS of thy name fills my heart when I forget mine — like thy morning sun when the mist is melted.

298

寧靜的夜晚有人母的美，喧嚷的白日有孩童的俏。

THE silent night has the beauty of the mother and the clamorous day of the child.

299

人微笑，世界愛他；人大笑，世界怕他。

THE world loved man when he smiled. The world became afraid of him when he laughed.

300

神等待人類憑靠智慧找回自己的童年。

GOD waits for man to regain his childhood in wisdom.

301

讓我感知這世界乃是祢的愛的化身，我的愛便會前來相助。

LET me feel this world as thy love taking form, then my love will help it.

302

祢的陽光對我心靈的冬天微笑，從不懷疑我的心田會有春花綻放。

THY sunshine smiles upon the winter days of my heart, never doubting of its spring flowers.

303

神以愛親吻有限；人以愛親吻不朽。

GOD kisses the finite in his love and man the infinite.

304

你穿越多少荒年，走過多少沙漠，方纔抵達完滿的那一瞬
間。

THOU crossest desert lands of barren years to reach the
moment of fulfilment.

305

神的緘默把人的思想催熟，化成言語。

GOD's silence ripens man's thoughts into speech.

306

永遠的旅人，你會發現我的詩篇處處有你的足跡無數。

THOU wilt find, Eternal Traveller, marks of thy footsteps
across my songs.

307

天父啊，祢將榮耀歸於祢的孩子，且讓我也爲祢爭光吧。

LET me not shame thee, Father, who displayest thy glory in
thy children.

308

天色陰鬱——烏雲深鎖眉頭，陽光像受罰的孩子，蒼白的
臉頰掛著數行清淚；風聲呼呼，像受了傷的世界的哭嚎。
但我知道我正走在路上，要去會見我的朋友。[31]

CHEERLESS is the day, the light under frowning clouds is
like a punished child with traces of tears on its pale cheeks,
and the cry of the wind is like the cry of a wounded world.
But I know I am travelling to meet my Friend.

309

滿月啊，今晚棕櫚樹葉搖曳，大海湧起波濤，宛如世界的心跳。你從哪一處不可知的天空，默默捎來愛情那令人心痛的祕密？

TO-NIGHT there is a stir among the palm leaves, a swell in the sea, Full Moon, like the heart throb of the world. From what unknown sky hast thou carried in thy silence the aching secret of love?

---

31 此詩最後一個詞 "my Friend" 以大寫表示。但是參照泰戈爾其他作品例如《吉檀迦利》，這裡的「朋友」並非普通意義的「朋友」，而是指神或梵。「朋友」這裡特以粗體字表示。

310

我夢見一顆星，一座光之島，那是我的出生地；在那裡，在生機勃發的悠閒生活中，我生命裡的所有工作將一一熟成，猶如秋陽遍照的稻田。[32]

I DREAM of a star, an island of light, where I shall be born and in the depth of its quickening leisure my life will ripen its works like the rice field in the autumn sun.

311

雨中的濕地揚起一股氣息，猶如沉默的升斗小民同聲合唱一首偉大的讚美詩。

THE smell of the wet earth in the rain rises like a great chant of praise from the voiceless multitude of the insignificant.

312

愛會落空，這是事實；但是我們不能把這事實視爲眞理。

THAT love can ever lose is a fact that we cannot accept as truth.

313

有朝一日我們將會了解：死亡永遠奪不走靈魂的收穫，因爲靈魂的收穫與靈魂自身相連，不可須臾離。

WE shall know some day that death can never rob us of that which our soul has gained, for her gains are one with herself.

---

32 泰戈爾這本詩集的語言讀來平易近人，但是在這首詩中他少見地用了一個很正式的字：quicken。這個字常見的意義是「使某事物加快或變快」（cause something to become quicker），例如「加快腳步」（to quicken our steps）。但是泰戈爾在這裡用的是另一個比較文言或正式的用法，即「使某事物變得更爲活躍或活潑」（cause something to become more active），因此這裡的 "its quickening leisure" 指的是敘述者「我」在該座光明之島上「生氣勃勃的閒暇生活」或「生意盎然的悠閒生活」。

314

神在暮色蒼茫中到訪，帶來我的昔日之花——那花安放在
祂的籃子裡，至今依然鮮麗。

GOD comes to me in the dusk of my evening with the flowers
from my past kept fresh in his basket.

315

神啊，一旦我的生命之弦全調好音，祢的每一觸動都會奏
出愛的樂章。

WHEN all the strings of my life will be tuned, my Master,
then at every touch of thine will come out the music of love.

316

神啊，讓我眞實地活著，惟其如此，死亡於我才會成爲眞實。[33]

LET me live truly, my Lord, so that death to me become true.

317

人類的歷史正耐心等待，等待那些受辱者贏得勝利。

MAN'S history is waiting in patience for the triumph of the insulted man.

---

33 這首詩玩了「真實地」（truly）與「真實」（true）的文字遊戲。就中譯而言，英文片語 "to become true" 譯成「成真」是更為簡潔，但這裡為了呼應前面的「真實地活著」（to live truly），因此選擇譯成「成為真實」。

318

此刻，我感覺你的目光落在我的心田，有如朝陽默默，落在秋收後荒涼的田疇。

I FEEL thy gaze upon my heart this moment like the sunny silence of the morning upon the lonely field whose harvest is over.

319

我渴望渡過這波濤洶湧的咆哮之海，抵達彼岸的詩歌之島。

I LONG for the Island of Songs across this heaving Sea of Shouts.

320

夜的序曲開始了——在落日的樂音中，在頌揚神奇暗夜的莊嚴聖歌裡。

THE prelude of the night is commenced in the music of the sunset, in its solemn hymn to the ineffable dark.

321

曾經我攀登高峰，在聲名那荒涼與貧瘠的高處我找不到蔽身之所；我的嚮導啊，在日色消失之前，請帶我進入幽靜的山谷，生命的果實將在那裡熟成金色的智慧。

I HAVE scaled the peak and found no shelter in fame's bleak and barren height. Lead me, my Guide, before the light fades, into the valley of quiet where life's harvest mellows into golden wisdom.

322

暮色蒼茫，萬物看來十分詭異——高塔的基座消失在黑暗裡，樹梢看來像斑斑墨跡。我要等待早晨，待我醒來，我將在晨光中看見你的城。

THINGS look phantastic in this dimness of the dusk — the spires whose bases are lost in the dark and treetops like blots of ink. I shall wait for the morning and wake up to see thy city in the light.

323

我曾受苦，我曾絕望，我也曾見識過死亡；但我很高興此刻我仍活在這偉大的世間。

I HAVE suffered and despaired and known death and I am glad that I am in this great world.

324

我生命裡有幾處空曠寧靜的所在；那幾處開放的空間讓我忙碌的日子得到陽光，獲得空氣。

THERE are tracts in my life that are bare and silent. They are the open spaces where my busy days had their light and air.

325

放了我吧，未竟的過往！別緊抱著我的背，讓我難以前行，難以赴死。

RELEASE me from my unfulfilled past clinging to me from behind making death difficult.

326

這是我最後的遺言：「我相信你的愛。」

LET this be my last word, that I trust in thy love.

譯者後記

文／余淑慧

　　泰戈爾（Rabindranath Tagore, 1861-1941）生於今日印度的加爾各答，是個早慧的詩人兼思想家，少年時代就被視為「孟加拉的雪萊」，這是大家耳熟能詳的美談。一九一○年，五十歲的他出版了英文詩集《吉檀迦利》（Gitanjali），這讓他在一九一三年拿下諾貝爾文學獎桂冠，成為第一個獲得這份殊榮的東方人。

成長於書香世家的泰戈爾

　　據泰戈爾自己描述，他從小就生活在創作的氛圍裡，熟習各式各樣的語文與藝術活動。他的曾祖父與祖父都是成功的企業家，在國內經營銀行與各種產業，在國外則有專屬的船隊與東印度公司長年維持海外的生意往來。泰戈爾的父親不但善於維持家業，本身也熱愛藝術、哲學、宗教與教育活動。為了維持傳統文化，他帶領家人過著《奧義書》指導下的宗教生活，但是他並不排斥西方文化，也鼓勵子女學習西方思想、文學與藝術，甚至送兒女到英國或美國留學。

　　據泰戈爾的回憶錄，他們家可說是當時孟加拉的文藝中心，時常出現各式各樣的集會，日夜都有詩人、學者、

演員、畫家、教育家等文化界人士到訪，而他的父兄也不時舉行哲學討論會、詩歌朗誦或戲劇表演等活動以饗賓客。泰戈爾是家中的幼子，他的十三位兄姐大都表現傑出，學有專精，例如他的大哥是著名的哲學家兼詩人，二哥留學英國，精通梵、英、孟加拉文，除了英譯了許多印度古典文學，也是第一個進入英國殖民政府任職的印度人。除此之外，他的其他兄姐也曾組織劇團，或陸續合辦好幾份報刊與雜誌，發表他們創作或翻譯的小說、劇本、詩歌或文學評論。

泰戈爾的英語創作與翻譯之路

在這樣的家庭環境中，泰戈爾的創作生涯開始得很早。幼時他首先跟著兄長習畫，八歲那年棄畫學詩，十三歲那年把《馬克白》譯成詩劇，在家人與賓客前上台發表。十四歲嘗試投稿給雜誌，發表詩作與詩評，並出版第一本詩集。十七歲已經開始定期投稿給雜誌，固定發表劇本、抒情詩、敘事詩、歌曲與文學評論。

可能是因為《吉檀迦利》的成功或諾貝爾文學獎的刺激，二十世紀的前面二十年裡，泰戈爾的創作出現了有趣的變化：他改變跑道，大量使用英文作為發表與創作的媒介。例如一九一三年那年，除了再版《吉檀迦利》之外，他另外出版了兩部英文詩集《園丁集》（*The Gardener*）和

《新月集》（*The Crescent Moon*）。一九一六年出版《探果集》（*Fruit Gathering*）與《漂鳥集》（*Stray Birds*），一九一八年則出版了《情人的禮物》（*Lover's Gift*）與《橫渡集》（*Crossing*）。除了詩，他一生中也寫了大量的英語散文、書信、演講稿等等。

　　《吉檀迦利》以及上述幾部英文詩集有時會被評論家視為泰戈爾的譯作而非創作，因為作品的內容大部分都可在他的孟加拉語著作裡找到類似的「原文」。但是，由於通常只是內容類似，或「譯文」比「原文」精簡或省略很多，因而出現了泰戈爾刪節、改寫或改譯自己的「原文」之討論。或謂泰戈爾的「翻譯」不夠忠實，多少違背其「原文」之類的說法。

原文？譯文？雙語的泰戈爾

　　原文與譯文勢不兩立，自古而然；出現上述說法其實也無可厚非。不過，如果我們回顧泰戈爾生活於其間的歷史空間，以及他個人的成長背景，也許我們可以找到其他路徑，來面對泰戈爾在創作上以雙語演出的問題。

　　首先，印度直到一九四七年才脫離英國的統治，換言之，泰戈爾生活一輩子的地方，嚴格來說應該稱之為「英屬印度孟加拉管轄區加爾各答」，再換言之，泰戈爾其實是個英屬殖民地作家。一般來說，在英屬殖民地生活過

的人，因爲日常生活中本來就必須面對兩種語言與兩種文化，因此有能力流利使用母語和英語的人所在多有，泰戈爾並非特例，他的二哥就是一個很好的例子。

再者，泰戈爾的家庭是一個新舊交替，傳統與現代並存的書香世家，他的父親雖然堅持教導子女誦習傳統梵典，但他也很重視兒女的現代語言（英文與孟加拉語）的教育。據泰戈爾的傳記記載，他才七、八歲就有兄長教他模仿華茲華斯來創作英詩。他初生之犢不怕虎，竟也眞的開始寫起英詩。從這一件小事，可知交叉並用英文與母語，在他家裡或他兄弟姊妹之間是一件再尋常不過的事。自幼的耳濡目染，加上在一八七八年到一八八〇年之間他甚至還親赴英國，念了兩年的英國文學，他有能力駕馭兩種語言，有能力以英文寫作也不足爲奇。綜合考量泰戈爾所處的歷史背景、殖民地帶給他的跨文化或跨語言的社會背景、兼容傳統與現代的日常家庭生活，以及他本身的雙語或多語的成長經驗，我覺得把這幾部作品視之爲英文原作並無不可。

除了認可泰戈爾的雙語能力，將其作品視爲原文之外，在翻譯研究上還有另一個取徑，亦即將他的英文作品視爲「自譯」（self translation），亦即作者本人用母語之外的語言所創作的作品。這是二十世紀譯學（Translation Studies）發展以來，學者針對翻譯作品本身之研究，從而

開發出來的研究面向之一。泰戈爾從小就譯寫不斷，有時寫，有時譯，有時既譯既寫，他這幾部英文作品其實可視爲自譯之作來加以研究。不過由於「自譯」現象的研究尚未成熟[1]，加上這也不是目前本文的關懷所在，所以目前比較簡便的方式，還是暫時把泰戈爾用英文寫的作品視爲原作。本書之中譯，即把《漂鳥集》視爲原作處理。

《漂鳥集》歷來的閱讀與譯介

　　前述幾部作品裡，《漂鳥集》和《新月集》最爲知名，早在二十世紀初期就陸續被譯成中文，進入中文世界，深深影響中文的詩歌寫作，創造了所謂的「小詩運動」[2]，例如冰心即坦承《春水》、《繁星》兩部作品之出版，是因爲讀了泰戈爾的小詩，得到靈感才開始創作的。

　　泰戈爾的詩集在中文世界不僅引介時間早，坊間歷來的譯本也不少。若以《漂鳥集》而論，據詩人莫渝統計，自一九二〇年代鄭振鐸首次以白話文完整譯介泰戈爾以

1　這是翻譯理論家巴斯奈特（Susan Bassnett）的說法。見 Susan Bassnett, *Translation Studies*（London and New York: Routledge, 2014）.

2　見莫渝，〈無限寬廣的遐想──泰戈爾新月集與飛鳥集閱讀筆記〉，收在鄭振鐸譯，《泰戈爾新月集·飛鳥集》（台北縣新店市：桂冠圖書股份有限公司，2004 年），頁 XII。

來，就一直有許多人不斷嘗試翻譯泰戈爾，其中著名的譯者計有：周策縱、糜文開、羅青、傅一勤、卓加真，這一名單當然也包含莫渝本人。如此不曾間斷的閱讀與譯介活動，據莫渝推測，其原因大致不外乎「試筆、學習、喜歡與認同的回應」。[3]

這點我深有同感。作為一個讀者，我在人生不同的階段裡，都曾或深或淺地讀過泰戈爾，尤其是《漂鳥集》。高中時，我記得我讀過同學送的中譯本，目的是了解人生哲理。大學時代我又讀了一次，那是從圖書館裡借的雙語對照版，為的是背幾句漂亮的英文，希望寫英文作文作業時可以派上用場。等我自己在大學裡教翻譯，偶爾也會翻出《漂鳥集》找幾個簡短的例子，目的是為了跟學生解釋中英文各自不同的體質，與各自不同的表現特色。例如中文是意合（hypotaxis）語言，注重隱性連貫，字與詞與句之間往往不需要連接詞類來加以連接；但是英文是形合（parataxis）語言，得運用大量連接詞或介系詞等形式手段來連接語詞和子句，以便構成句子等諸如此類技巧與表達的問題。

雖然我喜歡《漂鳥集》，也常用《漂鳥集》來練習與傳授翻譯技巧，但是真的接手翻譯《漂鳥集》，加入前述前輩譯者行列卻是個偶然。過去兩年裡，我因為生活極其忙碌，有家人要照顧，有教學的工作得顧及，時間上產生

嚴重的碎裂。換言之，我無法抽出一段較長的時間坐下來寫作或翻譯。然而作為一個翻譯教學者，理論上又不能與翻譯這個活動須臾離。在此情況下，《漂鳥集》一首首短短的，最多只有三、四行的詩，似乎是個很好的選擇，讓我每天都能做一點翻譯。因此在某次談話間，漫遊者總編輯李亞南女士問我要不要翻譯泰戈爾，我沒想太多就應承了下來。

從此我不論去哪裡，包包裡都帶著從網路列印下來的 *Stray Birds* 和筆記本。事實上，《漂鳥集》的大部分詩句，我都是在等待的零碎時間裡，一首一首慢慢地譯成：若不是在公車站或捷運站翻，就是在便利商店或咖啡店等候接送小孩的零碎時間當中譯成，至少初譯稿的產生是如此。有時我頗疑心，這些譯詩會不會散發漂泊的氣味，洩露我的行蹤，或我生命中那些流浪或離散的軌跡。

保留原詩形式與「詩法」的翻譯策略

《漂鳥集》共有三百二十五首詩，其中有抒情，有寫景，有詠物，還有一部份是近乎格言或警語的哲理詩。這些小詩看似容易，因為用字清淺，幾乎看不到深奧的單字；句構也清楚明瞭，近乎口語，沒有太多長句省略句倒

3　同前注。

裝句等。但是，等我真的動手譯了才知道困難重重。其中最難的，不是傳達泰戈爾「說甚麼」，而是琢磨泰戈爾的「怎麼說」，或他的「詩法」——畢竟詩人怎麼寫，有時候比寫甚麼更重要。泰戈爾在寫給友人布瑞吉（Robert Bridges）的信中也提到這一點，即他認為在文學作品裡，「表達的模式」（mode of expression）往往遠比「思想的豐富」（richness of thought）更有價值[4]。為了這個原因，這部《漂鳥集》首先嘗試保留原詩的形式，一行就是一行，兩行就兩行，不強行予以調整或分行。這麼做還另有一個歷史原因：畢竟這種少則一行，多則三行的文學形式，曾在中文詩歌史上創造了「小詩運動」。

另外，這部中譯也希望盡量保留泰戈爾的技法或「詩法」。整體來看，泰戈爾筆下的技法，常見的有對比、對話、擬人與譬喻等[5]，例如最知名的開篇第 1 首就用了很多對比，其中有物的對比（漂鳥對落葉），動作的對比（漂鳥的「飛離」對黃葉的「飄落」）等等（詳參內文註解）；第 12 首是一段跟海水與天空的對話；第 3 首與第 5 首分別把世界與大漠擬人化，使之化身為謙卑的情人。譬喻分為明喻與隱喻兩大類，兩者在這部集子裡俯拾即是，十分常見，如第 8 首把「她憂傷的臉」比喻為「夜雨」，縈繞在詩人的夢裡，「猶如夜雨淅淅瀝瀝」。以上這幾個技法前人已經談過許多，這裡不再贅述。

我想要特別點明的是：泰戈爾是個有自覺地生活在兩個文化裡的人，也是個學習能力很強的詩人；他既擅於學習英文的詩學技巧或英文的特色，也懂得從自己的文化傳統裡吸收養分。首先他很懂得利用英文的詩學技巧或特色來製造韻律或節奏。這一點表現在頭韻（alliteration）的使用、代名詞性別的區分、英文時態差異所產生的對比。所謂頭韻，意指兩個以上相鄰或密切相關的語詞，共同使用了同一個字母起首，例如第 47 首的 her silent steps of love，其中 silent 和 steps 相連且都以 s 開頭，這是嚴格的頭韻；又如第 45 首第二行的 When his weapons win he himself defeated 一句，其中 weapons 和 win 相連且都以 w 開頭，這也是嚴格的頭韻。不過如果我們仔細看這一句，發現間隔不遠的第一個字 when 也是以 w 開頭，這種情況在《漂鳥集》極為常見，我因此也把這現象寬算為用韻，如第 1 首的 stray birds of summer 裡，stray 和 summer 雖然隔了兩個字，也視之為押了 s 頭韻。又如第二行描寫落葉的兩個動詞 flutter and fall，flutter 與 fall 兩字以 and 相連，且兩字密切相關，因此也視之為用韻字。

4　這句話的英文如下：In pure literature it is very often that the mode of expression is of greater value than richness of thought.

5　詩人莫渝在〈無限寬廣的遐想〉一文中有很精彩的分析，見注 2，頁 VIII-XI。

整體來說，在密切相關且相隔不遠的字押以頭韻這一手法，泰戈爾在《漂鳥集》裡用得最多，但是用得很含蓄，如果沒把英文念出來有時還真的難以發現。這是因爲中文詩通常都押尾韻，熟習中文詩的讀者本來就比較難以察覺頭韻的存在。由於中文詩通常都不押頭韻，因此這個部份幾乎找不到適當的語詞來對譯。不過爲了照顧到泰戈爾選字的用心，如果可以的話，我們在中文翻譯時通常以尾韻來作爲補償。例如第 86 首：

　　"HOW far are you from me, O Fruit?"
　　"I am hidden in your heart, O Flower."

　　這首小詩以對話的形式呈現，用韻上分別有 far / from / fruit，若寬一點算，第二行的 flower 也可列入；另外就是第二行的 hidden 和 heart 互押了頭韻。中文無法再現這樣巧妙的音聲安排，於是讓第一行末結尾的「遠」與第二行末的「田」押韻，希望多少做一點韻的補償。如下：

「果子啊，你離我多遠？」
「花朵啊，我就藏在你心田。」

　　這樣的例子實在很多，幾乎每隔三、五首就出現一

次，這裡就不再贅述。除了用韻，泰戈爾也很擅於利用英文代名詞來呈現性別，展現並列或對比的美感，例如第4，29，72，78，93，94，107，120，137，140，172，234這幾首詩。這幾首詩譯成中文之後，有的可以自然保留代名詞所指涉的性別，例如第4，93，120，137，140，172，234首。我們看第4首：

IT is the tears of the earth that keep <u>her</u> smiles in bloom.
正是大地自己的淚，讓<u>她</u>常保笑靨如花。

　　但是有許多首就無法在中文裡自然地再現性別，除非刻意強調或重複一次名詞，例如第78首和第94首：

THE grass seeks <u>her</u> crowd in the earth.
The tree seeks <u>his</u> solitude of the sky.
小草在地上尋找 [她的] 同伴；
大樹往天空探求 [他的] 孤獨。

THE mist is like the earth's desire. It hides the sun for whom <u>she</u> cries.
雲霧就像大地的欲望，遮蔽了<u>大地</u>聲聲呼喚的太陽。

再來，泰戈爾偶爾也會利用英文的時態來呈現今昔對比，例如第 264 首詩：

THE little flower <u>lies</u> in the dust.
It <u>sought</u> the path of the butterfly.
小花如今躺在塵土裡，
她尋覓過蝴蝶的小徑。

這首詩的第一行動詞 lies 是現在式，表示小花躺在塵土裡是她此時此刻的狀態。第二行的動詞 sought 是 seek 的過去式，意謂小花會躺在塵土，裡是因為她之前尋找過蝴蝶的空中小徑。這裡把小花擬人化，而且借用了時態說明今昔的對比，由此顯示詩人可愛的解釋或想像。中文的文字本身無法如此簡潔地創造今昔對照，除非以增譯的方式或加字解釋（「如今」），否則幾乎無法翻譯這一句（詳參註解）。

多義的文字遊戲

《漂鳥集》另一個難對付的翻譯挑戰是文字遊戲。泰戈爾熟讀《奧義書》是眾所周知的事，若是如此，那麼他在《漂鳥集》展現的文字遊戲技巧，顯然來自印度古典詩歌的傳統。這裡所謂的文字遊戲，指運用字的多義性，

含蓄傳達語言的趣味與詩的意旨，或以同源字為基礎，然後加上前綴後綴等變化來製造韻律，並藉以說明事物或概念之間的聯繫，這是《奧義書》常用的文字技巧。其中最為人所知的，應該是《大森林奧義書》第二梵書記載的「三Da」故事；艾略特（T. S. Eliot）曾把這故事寫入《荒原》，不知這是否就是泰戈爾在《漂鳥集》展現文字遊戲的靈感始源？總之，這個故事提到創世主有三支後裔，即天神、凡人、阿修羅。天神、凡人和阿修羅都曾當過梵行者（學生），跟隨創世主學習。梵行期滿，臨別前，天神、凡人、阿修羅各自前來跟創世主請示。創世主只對他們各自說了一聲Da。天神、凡人、阿修羅因各有各的「器」或稟賦，因而產生三種不同的領會：天神聽到Da，認為自己該自制（dāmyate）；凡人聽到Da，認為自己該佈施（data）；阿修羅聽了Da，認為自己該仁慈（dayadhvam）。對dāmyate、data、dayadhvam這三種答案，創世主全都予以首肯，認為他們都理解了。故事末了，天國之聲（即雷鳴）發出三聲：「Da! Da! Da!」以示呼應，意謂聽完故事的人應當學會自制、佈施與仁慈。

在《漂鳥集》裡，我們不時也會發現這種從一個字變化出好幾個字的技巧，有時在一行裡出現兩個同形字，例如第56首：

LIFE is given to us, we earn it by giving it.
生命是天賜的禮物；我們藉由奉獻生命，獲得這份贈禮。

　　其中的 given 和 giving 來自動詞 give，意指「被給予」和「給予／付出」。有時則多達三個，例如第 111 首的 ends，ending 和 endless：

THAT which ends in exhaustion is death, but the perfect ending is in the endless.
倦怠的止盡處是死亡，完美的止盡處是無止無盡。

　　這裡有三個同形字，中譯很努力嘗試，目前似乎也只能做到兩個對應：「止盡處」與「無止無盡」（詳參註解）。翻譯理論家勒弗維爾（André Lefevere）認為詩的這種文字遊戲通常是不可譯的，只能想別的辦法來創造字與字，觀念與觀念，或意象與意象之間的關連。誠哉斯言！

　　在這部集子裡，使用此技巧的詩尚有好幾首，例如第24，56，57，60，62，129，130，150，159，176，184，208，228，254，316首等等。有的湊巧能找到兩組可以對應的語詞對譯，有的只能罷手興嘆，只好期待他日或有高手出現，想出辦法，見招拆招，一一化解這些文字的結。

最後要說的是，這部小小的詩集的初譯稿固然出自我手，但是由於一個人的學力與精力有限，因此初稿謄繕完畢，去年暑假期間即交由舍妹淑娟潤稿。淑娟過去頗有一點翻譯經驗，潤校之餘，有時也附上許多建議，提供許多譯詞或譯句。有些譯詞譯句我實在很喜歡，就直接採用，因此這集子裡有許多詩可說是我們姊妹的合譯。例如第44首：

THE world rushes on over the strings of the lingering heart making the music of sadness.

紅塵倥傯，在徬徨不捨的心上奏起憂傷的樂音。

　　這裡前半行是淑娟的手筆，後半段是我的翻譯。又如第71首：

THE woodcutter's axe begged for its handle from the tree.

The tree gave it.

樵夫的斧頭向大樹討根斧柄。

大樹慨然應允。

　　這裡又顛倒過來，第一行是我的，第二行則是淑娟的。如此的例子很多。潤稿收回來後，我花了半年七校其稿，

這之後，再也無法分辨是譯是潤，因而同時掛名。

除了謝謝淑娟大力幫忙，這份詩稿的完成，我另外必須謝謝編輯貝雯的耐心等待，細心校閱，並提供許多修改的意見。序文方面也要感謝貝雯適時插入小標題，幫我分章別目，讓全文眉目頓時清晰許多。另外，我還要感謝女兒茂嘉從四校到七校的過程裡，每一次都幫我找出錯別字或掉字冗字等等問題。四校的階段她還是個高中生，如今已經是大學新鮮人，這部詩稿和泰戈爾還真的陪我們走了很長的一段路。

漂鳥集
Stray Birds

作　者	泰戈爾(Rabindranath Tagore)
譯　者	余淑慧、余淑娟
內 頁 插 圖	liaoweigraphic
內 頁 構 成	呂德芬
美 術 設 計	呂德芬
內 頁 排 版	高巧怡
行 銷 企 劃	蕭浩仰、江紫涓
行 銷 統 籌	駱漢琦
業 務 發 行	邱紹溢
營 運 顧 問	郭其彬
責 任 編 輯	張貝雯、林芳吟
總 編 輯	李亞南
出　版	漫遊者文化事業股份有限公司
地　址	台北市103大同區重慶北路二段88號2樓之6
電　話	(02) 2715-2022
傳　真	(02) 2715-2021
服 務 信 箱	service@azothbooks.com
網 路 書 店	www.azothbooks.com
臉　書	www.facebook.com/azothbooks.read

發　行	大雁出版基地
地　址	新北市231新店區北新路三段207-3號5樓
電　話	(02) 8913-1005
訂 單 傳 真	(02) 8913-1056
初 版 一 刷	2024年8月
定　價	台幣299元

ISBN　978-986-489-982-1

國家圖書館出版品預行編目 (CIP) 資料

漂鳥集 / 泰戈爾(Rabindranath Tagore)
著 ; 余淑慧, 余淑娟譯. -- 二版. -- 臺北市
: 漫遊者文化事業股份有限公司出版 : 大
雁出版基地發行, 2024.08
　面；　公分
中英對照賞析譯註版
譯自 : Stray birds
ISBN 978-986-489-982-1(精裝)
867.51　　　　　　　　　　113010389

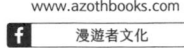
漫遊，一種新的路上觀察學
www.azothbooks.com
漫遊者 f 漫遊者文化

大人的素養課，通往自由學習之路
www.ontheroad.today
遍路文化
on
the road
f 遍路文化·線上課程